DAWN OF HELL

After the Great Destruction, when the nations of earth had finally brought their civilization to dust, there remained, unharmed, a group of apes and humans. This group, led from the ruins into the wilderness by the mighty ape Caesar, founded their own new world: The City of the Apes.

Caesar saw this new world as an arboreal Eden, a place where apes ruled benevolently, where apes learned man's ways and bettered them, knew man's savageries and avoided them.

But Caesar was wrong. What he couldn't see until too late was the future, the terrifying truth that awaited him in the rubble of the old city. The inevitable. The time when man would rise and fight again—and ape would slaughter ape. . . .

BATTLE FOR THE PLANET OF THE APES

David Gerrold

Screenplay by
John William Corrington
and Joyce Hooper Corrington

Copies of this printing
distributed in the United Kingdom by
Universal-Tandem Publishing Company, Ltd.

AWARD BOOKS
NEW YORK

*For Harlan Ellison,
who will appreciate the thought.*

AWARD BOOKS are published by
Universal-Award House, Inc., a subsidiary of
Universal Publishing and Distributing Corporation,
235 East Forty-fifth Street, New York, N.Y. 10017

Manufactured in the United States of America

BATTLE FOR THE PLANET
OF THE APES

PROLOGUE

Many years, many centuries, after the fact, an orangutan sat on a hillside and taught a class. He read to his students from a large handwritten book. And in this manner does history become legend and legend become myth.

"In the beginning, God created Beast and Man, so that both might live in friendship and share dominion over a world at peace.

"But in the fullness of time evil men betrayed God's trust and, in disobedience to His holy word, waged bloody wars not only against their own kind but also against the apes, whom they reduced to slavery.

"Then God in his wrath sent the world a savior, miraculously born . . ."

The time of the Savior was a time when the world needed a savior.

The surface of the Earth had been ravaged by the vilest war in human history. The great cities of *the world had been split asunder and were flattened.*

Out of one such city came a remnant of apes and men who had survived. History would report that they came in search of a place where Ape and Human might live together in friendship. But their thoughts were of survival, not of friendship.

And after survival, retribution.

One does not live peacefully with one's former oppressors. One punishes. One seeks vengeance.

And that was their mistake. The apes had brought the ways of evil men with them. The apes were proud that they had thrown off the yoke, but they failed to realize that they had not thrown it away. They put men into it and made them live in shame.

They adopted other ways of men, too. Like men, they quarreled among themselves. Like men, they argued over directions and goals. Like men, they forgot their original purposes.

And like men, they paid homage to strength.

When the apes planted their orchards and sowed their fields, they also planted fruits of bitterness and sowed seeds of discontent.

That crop would soon be ready for harvest.

One among them might be a savior—but like other saviors before him, he had to find a way to make his people listen . . .

ONE

Aldo the gorilla knew how to save his people.

Aldo the gorilla had a plan. It was a good plan. It was right. He knew it. He smacked his lips in anticipation as he thought of it. Yes. Apes should be strong. Apes should be masters. Apes should be proud. Apes should make the Earth shake when they walked.

Apes should *rule* the Earth.

He knew that someday they would. And he would be the gorilla who would lead them to victory.

He sat on his horse, on a ridge, and stared out over the desert below. Somewhere out there was a city . . . or what was left of it. Perhaps there were men there, too. Dangerous men. With guns. And bombs. Apes should be ready for them. Apes should kill them.

The thought excited him. He leaned forward in the saddle eagerly, squinting and frowning. Was there something out there? The city was forbidden, but the thought was so alluring . . .

But now was not the time. Not yet, not yet.

He snorted loudly and kicked his horse in the ribs to make it move. He pulled hard on the reins and wheeled the animal around. He trotted toward the gorilla outpost farther along the ridge.

The gorillas came to attention, grumbling. They were slovenly and untidy, and that made Aldo glad—it was a sign of their strength. As he rode through their ranks, they saluted, and he grinned in response.

He kept on going and headed down the side of the ridge, away from the desert, toward a valley that was startling in its sudden lushness so close to the blasted sand. The valley was deep and peaceful. Vineyards, fields of crops, clusters of trees—Aldo grunted, restless at the sight. There was so little challenge there.

He kicked the horse again, urging it faster. He splashed through a shallow stream. Ahead lay Ape City, nestled in the midst of dense trees. It was an arboreal city, multilevel, with numerous tree houses blending in with the forest around. Vines and ladders hung from openings to permit easy entry, and there were limbs that could be climbed from one level to another. Food hung outside the windows, all vegetables and fruit. Flowers grew in suspended pots. The whole vista was one of tranquillity.

Aldo sneered in annoyance. Kicking his horse once more, he galloped at full speed down into the valley, along a narrow road, through a grove of trees leading into Ape City. The wind lashed against his face; the dust of the road made his eyes water, and he squinted in reflex. But he galloped along, anyway, for the sheer brutal joy of it. The feel of the horse's hooves pounding along the dirt was rhythmic and powerful.

He came loudly around a curve in the road and reined in suddenly. A wagon had collapsed, blocking his way. His horse reared up at the sudden stop; Aldo jerked the bridle viciously, holding the animal in fierce control. It pulled nervously to one side and whinnied in protest, but Aldo ignored it.

One of the wheels had come off the wagon. Overloaded with fruit and vegetables, it rested on the blunt end of its axle. Four human males in identical brown homespun tunics were trying to raise it; they were all unshaven and longhaired.

Off to one side stood a black man Aldo knew as MacDonald; he held a clipboard and a sheaf of papers in his hands. He was looking concerned—more about the broken wagon than about the delay he was causing Aldo.

Aldo snorted. He dismounted and strode over to the wagon. He grabbed hold of it with one hand and lifted; he gestured to the men to replace the wheel, holding the wagon up easily until they were done.

One of them, a broad-shouldered, golden-haired young man named Jake, grinned, "Thanks, Aldo. You've got the strength of a gorill . . . oh, sorry." He stopped himself as he caught the darkening expression on Aldo's face.

Was it an insult? Aldo snarled. Though Jake was tall and muscular, Aldo towered over him; he slapped Jake's face hard with a huge, hairy hand.

"Man is *weak!*" He slapped him again, the sound of it cracked in the air. "Man is *weak!* And you will address me by my rank of general!"

Jake glared at him in a long, tense silence. It was broken finally by MacDonald. "Yes, General." He said it in a deadpan monotone.

Aldo contemptuously pushed Jake aside and remounted his horse. He rode off quickly.

Jake spat after him, "That gorilla makes me sick."

MacDonald nodded. "I'll speak to Caesar."

"What good will that do? Nobody can control Aldo."

The black man shrugged. "We can try." But he realized the truth of Jake's words. He stared off down the road at the rapidly retreating Aldo; Aldo was dangerous, he knew it; he had seen the signs in too many men not to recognize them in the gorilla.

Aldo rode recklessly into Ape City. Apes and humans dodged out of his way as he clattered through the avenues.

In the nine years since its founding, Ape City had established a culture of its own. Apes were the dominant class, humans the servants, though not physically ill treated. Humans could be seen carrying lumber and parcels, sweeping, doing laundry, tending ape children, and building shacks below the tree houses of their masters.

Apes wore uniforms, green and black and tan. Humans wore faded tunics, the same tunics that had been worn by their ape slaves half a generation before.

Aldo pulled his horse up to a hitching post and

dismounted. It was good that apes were the masters—but they weren't firm enough with their
slaves. Ape and human children were playing in the
streets; apes were riding humans, tossing them
things to fetch, and treating them affectionately,
like puppies. That was wrong—it might teach ape
children to be too lenient with humans. It might
even teach apes to *like* humans. He growled deep in
his throat at the thought.

Aldo strode through the street toward a building
set on the ground. It was the ape school. Aldo
hated it.

Inside, the room was large enough to permit the
simultaneous teaching of two classes without either
interfering with the other—unless voices were un-
duly raised; as sometimes happened.

In one class, an earnest but amiable bespectacled
human was teaching reading and writing, speaking
to a class self-segregated into two groups: in front
sat child chimpanzees and child orangutans; in the
rear sat the more backward gorillas—both children
and adults. They looked sullen and truculent in
their black leather uniforms.

The other class was less a class than what a university might have called a tutorial. Three adoles-
cent apes—two chimpanzees and one orangutan—
sat raptly at the feet of a young orangutan named
Virgil. Virgil was an intellectual prodigy whose
witty and fluent speech could only just keep pace
with the ideas that fizzed in his remarkable brain.

Both Teacher—for that was the name the apes
had given him—and Virgil were equipped with
chalk stone to write on two chipped old chalkboards

salvaged from the dead city. Their pupils wrote with charcoal sticks on skin parchment or papyrus. If pens, pencils, and paper still existed, they were reserved for the elite.

Aldo surveyed the scene with ill-concealed annoyance. Particularly the human-taught class. Humans teaching apes, indeed! Teacher had just finished chalking up the words "APE SHALL NEVER KILL APE" on the board. The chimp and orangutan children watched attentively. But behind them the gorillas were restless and mumbled to each other.

Teacher turned to the class. "Gorillas! Read me what I have written."

There was glazed incomprehension and silence from the back row.

Teacher sighed. Then, more hopefully: "Orangutans? Chimpanzees?"

In unison, the front row recited, "Ape shall never kill Ape!"

Aldo moved into the classroom then to stand beside his usual place on the front bench. The class fell silent as he entered. Aldo eyed the teacher and growled, "Can Ape ever kill Man?"

There was a growl of approval from the gorillas in the back. As it subsided, Teacher said coldly, ignoring his question, "You're late, General Aldo. Again." He wrote something into a battered book he held.

"What are you writing?" demanded Aldo.

Teacher extended the book. "Come and read it. To the class."

"I won't," the gorilla said sullenly.

"You won't," Teacher chided gently, "because you can't. And you can't, because you don't want to learn." He shut the book. "And it's my duty to tell that to Caesar."

Aldo's growl was silenced by the word "Caesar," which also prompted an alert little boy chimpanzee to rise to his feet. He said wistfully, "If my father were a gorilla, we'd all be learning riding instead of writing."

The gorillas howled appreciatively. All the apes laughed, chimpanzees and orangutans too.

Teacher smiled kindly. "Cornelius," he said to the boy chimp, "Remember you're Caesar's son and heir. Being a good rider won't make you a good ruler. Although," he added drily, "in human history, quite a number of monarchs—and military dictators—seem to have thought that was enough." He looked at Aldo as he said this last. He turned back to the class. "Now all of you take your charcoal sticks and copy down what I've written. The best shall be hung from this hook on the wall."

Aldo took his place grumbling and eyeing the teacher. "I can think of better things to hang from hooks."

He picked up his charcoal stick clumsily and began to make marks on the papyrus. It was difficult; he looked around to see if anyone else was having problems. The chimpanzees and orangutans were writing clearly and rapidly; the other gorillas were working slowly and with difficulty. Aldo bent back to his papyrus; he pressed harder, as if that would help. The charcoal stick snapped in two. "Aaargh!" he snarled. He hated the school! He hated writing!

It was a useless waste of time—it was an occupation fit only for men! And for the weaker apes, chimpanzees and orangutans! "Effete intellectuals," he fumed; they weren't much better than humans!

In cheerful contrast, at the classroom's other end, the young orangutan Virgil was stimulating the minds of his three ape pupils. He was trying to exercise their brains with argument, not fill them with facts. The dialogue was quick tempoed.

"But, Virgil, can we *alter* destiny? Can we tamper with time?"

Virgil's smile was mischievous. "Accept my premise, and I will prove it logically."

"What premise?"

"That the legends are true—that Man learned to travel not only faster than sound but faster than light as well."

"All right, we accept the premise."

"Then imagine a musician giving a live broadcast from what was once London to what was once New York on a Wednesday. He then travels faster than light from London to New York, where he arrives on the previous Tuesday, listens to his own broadcast on Wednesday, dislikes its quality intensely, and travels back faster than light to London in time to talk himself out of giving the broadcast in the first place."

The chimpanzees and the orangutan shouted with laughter at this dubious but invigorating idea.

On the other side of the room, Teacher heard the happy laughter and envied it; that was what teaching should be. He sighed and went on mechanically scrutinizing and stacking on the desktop the parchments that the last of the chimp and orangutan children were now submitting for his inspection. "That's very good, Mirko. You're dismissed."

Cornelius was the last of the chimps to present his parchment. Teacher looked it over carefully. "Good, Cornelius ... Oh, there's a mistake. You've written a 'B' for the second 'P.' 'APE SHALL NEXER KILL ABE.' " He smiled jovially, "Who's Abe?"

There was a pause. Then Cornelius said softly, "Teacher, have you forgotten your own name?"

Teacher was startled—and then touched. His eyes became moist. His voice fell to a whisper, and he mused, almost to himself, "So many people call me 'Teacher,' I'd almost . . ." He smiled at the chimp. " 'Ape shall never kill Abe.' Thank you, Cornelius. That was a very kind thought." He pulled himself together with visible effort. "You're dismissed." Cornelius trotted out.

He stood up and looked toward the back of his class. "Gorillas! Are you done?" He stared at them as firmly as he could; they were so much like children; discipline was all they understood. It was a shame their bodies had matured before their minds. With their incredible strength to force things to their will, they had no incentive to learn; they could accomplish what they wanted by the most direct—and brutal—method.

The gorillas were hunched, motionless yet menacing, on their back-row benches. Aldo rose from his place and slouched insolently toward Teacher. He slapped his parchment on the desktop beside the others.

Teacher picked it up and scrutinized it. "General Aldo, with respect, this is barely legible and will have to be written again. Your capital 'A' leans over like a tent in a high wind, and your 'K' is . . ."

Aldo curled his lip. Glaring at Teacher, he deliberately took Cornelius' parchment from the top of the pile and began to tear it into shreds.

Teacher shouted at him, agonized, "No, Aldo! No!"

Abruptly, every ape in the room froze, shocked into hostility. Aldo turned apoplectic. The gorillas sprang to their feet in menacing unison. Virgil, appalled, raced across the schoolroom floor. "Teacher!" he cried. "You've spoken the unspeakable! You've said 'No' to an ape!"

Teacher went pale, shocked with the realization of what he had done.

"Teacher!" said Virgil. "You know better—you know why a human must never, *never*, say 'No' to an ape. In all our years of slavery to men, the word 'No' was the one word apes were electrically conditioned to fear. Caesar has forbidden men to utter it ever. An ape may say 'No' to a human. But a human may never again say 'No' to an ape!" He stepped in closer and whispered, "Tell them you're sorry, Abe, and go home while you still have a home to go to. I'll try to put in a word for you with Caesar."

Teacher nodded slowly and turned to the gorillas. "I . . . I'm sorry. The writing you destroyed was by Caesar's son. I ... did not want you to suffer Caesar's anger."

Aldo snarled at the name. "What do I care for Caesar's anger? Let me give you a taste of mine!"

The big gorilla lifted up a block of wood and hurled it at Teacher's head. Taking their cue, the other gorillas began to run joyfully amok, roaring and screaming. They overturned Teacher's desk and ripped up the papyruses. And then they headed for Teacher.

Teacher ran from the classroom. The gorillas boiled after him like bees swarming out of a hive. He lurched out into the street, stumbled, caught his footing and ran. The gorillas chased after him, and the rest of the students, seeing the excitement, came tailing after.

Teacher panted as he ran—he wasn't used to this kind of exercise—his lungs ached from the effort; he charged through stalls of fruit and vegetables. The gorillas came barrelling after, upsetting baskets and tables. Aldo was in the lead, shouting and roaring. The shoppers and stall-tenders screamed as they leapt out of his way.

Teacher dodged and whirled, around a house, down a street. There, ahead of him! There was a work area where humans were plaiting screen walls for houses. Maybe he could hide there! But the gorillas had already seen him. They came crashing through the screens after him.

Teacher tried to hold onto his glasses as he ran. He took off again, this time in a different direction—toward Caesar's house. Caesar would help him!

But he wasn't fast enough. Aldo came roaring down on him like a freight train and threw him roughly to the ground, pushing him into the dirt.

Grinning fiercely, Aldo drew his sword from his belt. It was broad and flat and short. He raised it high over his head.

Teacher tried to raise one arm in protest. Apes and humans alike gasped in shock.

And then someone, *an ape*, cried, "Stop!"

All heads whirled to look—it was Caesar, standing in his doorway. He was a tall, strong chimpanzee; he had the bearing of a leader. Just behind him stood MacDonald, his chief human adviser.

The gorillas stared at Caesar. Aldo glared sullenly at him, his sword still raised over Teacher.

Caesar stepped down from the doorway, his stare fiercer than Aldo's. "I said . . . stop . . . Aldo."

Their eyes locked. Aldo burned with a fierce red anger, but Caesar's quieter strength was more effective. Aldo averted his eyes. He looked around for support, but there was none from the other gorillas; they were too thoroughly cowed by Caesar's authority. And there was certainly none from any of the chimpanzees and orangutans in the crowd; they were eyeing the gorillas with cold disdain and Caesar with love and respect.

At last, slowly, Aldo lowered his sword. But he waved in the direction of the Teacher, shouting his frustration. "He broke the Law! With his own mouth he broke the First Law!"

Caesar seemed to grow. "*I* am the Law," he said sternly. "And if I find that he has broken it, *I* shall pass judgment. What has he done?"

Virgil pushed forward through the crowd. "I can tell you. I was there."

Caesar turned to him, his tone softening, "Yes, Virgil . . . ?"

"I was there," Virgil said breathlessly; he too was still panting from the chase. "Teacher only . . . only . . . reverted to type under provocation. He spoke like a slave master from the old days of servitude. He spoke the negative imperative used for the conditioning of mechanical obedience."

Caesar smothered a smile. MacDonald grinned broadly. Caesar said, "Put that in words which even Caesar can understand."

"He said, 'No, Aldo, no!' "

The crowd gasped at that, the apes in anger, the humans in fear.

MacDonald stepped forward and began to help Teacher up. "Teacher, you're old enough to be well aware that 'No' is the one word a human may never say to an ape, because apes once heard it said to them a hundred times a day by humans."

"Yes," Teacher nodded. "I am old . . . enough."

"Then what was the provocation?"

Teacher was uneasy. He swallowed hard. He looked back and forth between Caesar, Aldo, and MacDonald. Finally, he managed to say, "General Aldo tore up a writing exercise written especially for me by Caesar's son. It was very good and . . . respectfully affectionate."

Caesar turned to Aldo and confronted him. "Why did you tear it up?"

Aldo sullenly refused to answer. From the crowd,

a young chimpanzee called, "Because Teacher said that the general's writing was very bad."

The chimpanzees and orangutans in the crowd laughed. The gorillas didn't; they fumed in silent embarrassment, and one or two curled their lips in anger.

Caesar said, after a pause, "General Aldo is a very good rider. My son is not, though he wishes to be. But my son *is* a very good writer. General Aldo is not. Apes cannot excel at everything," he said, smiling obliquely at Virgil, "with very few exceptions. That is all there is to it. The matter will be forgotten. Now go back to school."

"The schoolroom has been wrecked, Caesar," Virgil said. "By the gorillas."

Aldo snorted triumphantly. "Class ended! Schoolroom closed! Now we go back to riding horses!" There was an approving bark from the gorilla group behind him, but it was quickly checked as Caesar advanced to within an inch of the general's face.

Caesar's voice was firm. "You and your 'friends' will go back and put the schoolroom in order."

Their eyes locked. Aldo glared back, not quite totally defiant, not yet. He fumed, but he sheathed his sword.

Caesar turned on his heel and headed back toward his house, summoning MacDonald to his side with a curt gesture.

MacDonald caught up to him, frowning. This might be a good time to broach the subject of what happened on the road. He offered, "Caesar, I think that Aldo's hatred is not confined to humans."

Caesar was charitable; he shrugged it off. "Aldo still remembers the old days."

MacDonald couldn't be that charitable. "I think he'd like to bring them back."

Caesar looked at him curiously, but he did not ask the man to explain his odd remark.

TWO

Caesar's house was large and airy, its architectural style simple and clean. It was decorated with wood and paper and plaited screens. The impression was that of a rich tropical forest brought indoors.

Caesar's wife, Lisa, a pretty young chimpanzee, was preparing a meal of fruit, nuts, and vegetables for her husband and his adviser, MacDonald. A young, attractive serving girl was working with her.

Occasionally, Lisa would cast a motherly glance out the window. Directly outside was a collection of swings, vines, and perches on which Cornelius was playing with a human boy.

At the moment, Cornelius was poised on a perch. "Hey, Jimmy, d'you want to play follow-my-leader?" And with that, he executed a series of complicated flips, landing easily on a lower limb.

Jimmy watched sourly. When Cornelius stopped and looked at him questioningly, he made a disgusted face. "No. You're always the leader." He reached down and picked up a stick about rifle length; he pointed it at Cornelius, "Tchang, tchang! I got you!"

Cornelius clutched his breast, fell backward off the limb to the ground, uttering a loud cry of agony.

Almost immediately, Lisa stuck her head out the window. Seeing Cornelius lying on the ground, she hurried outside. "Cornelius, are you hurt?"

Cornelius rolled over and opened his eyes. He looked up at her. "No, Mother. I'm just dead."

"Dead?"

At this, Jimmy hid the makeshift gun behind his back, then dropped it quietly to the ground.

Cornelius grinned and explained, "We were playing gorillas."

Lisa frowned. First at her son, then at Jimmy. Was this human child teaching Cornelius bad habits? Jimmy sidled off backward, looking ashamed and defensive. "You were playing what?" she asked.

Cornelius stood up. "We were playing war."

"War?" Now Lisa *was* upset. She straightened abruptly. The sudden motion startled Jimmy. Already thoroughly intimidated, he turned and ran. Lisa watched him go in annoyance, then turned back to her son. She spoke icily. "Cornelius, hasn't your father explained to you many times that war isn't a game, except to pear-shaped old generals sticking colored pins in a map three thousand miles behind the firing lines?"

Cornelius looked properly abashed. "Yes, Mother."

"And hasn't he forbidden you to play with guns or to make a game of killing?"

"Yes, Mother."

"Then you'll stop it?"

"Yes, Mother."

Satisfied, Lisa turned and reentered the house. Caesar and MacDonald had come in while she was dealing with Cornelius. They had seated themselves at the dining room table and were talking quietly. Lisa moved to help the serving girl finish the dinner preparations.

MacDonald was saying, "You handled that situation with Aldo very adroitly, Caesar."

Caesar sighed and shook his head. "I wish I had been *educated* to be a ruler."

MacDonald looked puzzled. Didn't Armando...?"

Caesar shook his head again. "My dear, dead human foster-father—when he wasn't training me to be a bareback rider in his circus—taught me the sum of all human virtues. Which is that we must love one another or die. The lion-tamer was allowed to crack his whip, provided he didn't whip the lion."

"And if the lion attacked the tamer?"

"The lion never did. That's how I thought it would be in the world outside. If my father and mother had only lived, they might have taught me whether it was right to kill an evil enemy so that good should prevail."

"Well," said MacDonald. "History shows . . ."

Caesar cut him off sharply. "Human history! Not ape history. Ape never kills ape!"

Chastened, MacDonald shut up.

Caesar said, a little more slowly, reaching out to his friend, "We are making a new kind of world, MacDonald. We cannot replace one master with another; we must do away with those old human ideas of masters and slaves altogether. There must be no killing, no violence, no oppression of any kind. Human history says it's all right to kill. Apes must make a new kind of history, and we have no precedents to guide us, man friend."

MacDonald bit his lip; he wanted to speak but was holding himself back. He knew that Caesar was wrong on this point. There had been good men and noble precedents in human history—there would always be good men; apes could not have freed themselves without the help of good men. MacDonald's own brother had once aided Caesar, saved him from the governor of the city.

But there was no way he could convince Caesar that there were noble precedents in human history. Caesar was convinced he was bringing a new idea to the world. MacDonald sighed to himself. He wished he could get it through to the chimpanzee that what he thought was new thinking was only ignorance of the past.

Lisa brought the food to the table then. The bowls were rough cut out of wood, as was the table, almost refectory style. She and the serving girl placed the meal, totally vegetarian, before the chimpanzee and the man.

MacDonald took advantage of the interruption to try to change the mood. He exclaimed hungrily, "Mmm, I could eat a horse."

Lisa stopped in startlement and looked at him. "A horse?"

Caesar looked up, realizing her misconception, and joked, "You remember, Lisa. They used to eat all sorts of things—dead cattle, dead chickens, dead pigs, dead fish. . . ."

"Fish I can understand, just barely," said Lisa. "But *horses!* If horses, why not hippos? Where do you draw the line?"

MacDonald sighed. He took a nut and looked knowingly at the serving girl. She caught his look but turned away. Caesar was watching. MacDonald crunched the nut slowly while thinking what to say. He'd been through this argument before with other apes. Chimpanzees and orangutans couldn't understand that human beings *liked* meat, that meat was one of the foods that men needed because they had evolved to need it. He muttered, "If there were any hippos around, Lisa, they would be safe now. Now we eat fruits and nuts at our master's command."

Caesar frowned. "We are not your masters," he said angrily.

MacDonald was unabashed. He looked calmly back at Caesar. "We're not your equals."

Caesar did not take it as a rebuke. The remark had not been intended as such. He returned MacDonald's even stare. "MacDonald, I believe that when you come truly to know and trust a person as I know and trust you, you can't help but like him. Once my people come to know and trust yours, we shall all become equals and stay so . . . until the end of the world."

MacDonald nodded glumly. "That may be sooner than you think."

The statement caused an abrupt silence. Lisa was just dismissing the serving girl, but she turned to stare. Caesar paused with his hand halfway to his mouth. Something about the way MacDonald had said it . . . "You're a pessimist." But he said it without force.

"Or a prophet," corrected MacDonald.

Lisa came back to the table smiling. "You've been at the fermented coconut milk again," she chided. "They say it makes you very happy at night and very gloomy in the morning."

"Now that apes are at the helm," Caesar said, "Earth will sail safely through space until the end of time. And Virgil says that time is circular, that it has no end." Caesar declared almost petulantly, "I don't believe what you say."

"Would you believe it if you heard it from the lips of your own parents?" Almost immediately MacDonald regretted saying the words.

Caesar looked at him stunned. "That's not possible." And then, "Is it?"

MacDonald bit his lip. He had said too much already.

"*Is it?*" demanded Caesar. "Is it possible?"

MacDonald nodded, almost imperceptibly, and whispered, "It is."

Caesar leaped to his feet, and his chair fell behind him with a crash. He leaned over the table toward MacDonald. "Are my parents still alive?"

"No. But their images and their voices are."

"MacDonald, don't talk in riddles! Can I see

them? Can I hear them? Armando told me only that they came out of the future. Can they give me ... *knowledge?*"

MacDonald straightened up. There was no way to hide this from Caesar. And he did have a right to know. "You can see them," he said. "And you can hear them. And they can give you knowledge."

"How?"

"Under the dead city," the man explained, "in the archives near the old command post, there are tapes, sealed tapes of Cornelius and Zira being examined by officials of the American government. When my brother was Governor Breck's assistant, he told me about them. I know where they are. And I know that they concern Earth's future, from which your parents came."

"But the city was flattened. The bombs left nothing."

MacDonald's face creased thoughtfully, the black skin wrinkling into a frown. "The archives section—indeed, many sections of the underground city—were designed to survive the impact of a ten-megaton blast. I suspect ..." he let the sentence trail off.

But Caesar caught his meaning anyway. "Then the tapes and the pictures of my parents...."

"Yes," MacDonald said. "They might still be down there."

Caesar was excited now. "I want to see what they looked like, MacDonald. I want to hear what they thought and knew."

"The city is still radioactive."

Caesar waved that away in annoyance. "I want

to go anyway. Besides, who among your people knows anything about radioactivity?"

MacDonald sighed. Most of the real scientists had been killed nine years ago in the ape uprising. "No one," he admitted.

"And," chided Caesar, "among my people, is there one?"

MacDonald knew what Caesar was driving at. "Who knows everything about everything?"

"Right. Go find Virgil." Caesar made a decision. "We will leave before dawn."

MacDonald nodded in acquiescence. He didn't like it, he didn't want to go, but he knew that Caesar would not be satisfied until he had found the truth about his parents and his future. Virgil, of course, would be delighted—Virgil was always pleased at the prospect of discovering new knowledge. But MacDonald had misgivings. He didn't know why, but he felt uneasy about the whole venture. Perhaps it was because of the danger—not to himself, but to Caesar and to Ape City. If anything were to happen to the chimpanzee leader, there would be no one; there would be nothing to stop General Aldo from taking over.

And if that happened, it would not be good for anyone. Not for humans, not for chimpanzees, not for orangutans. Only for General Aldo and his gorillas.

MacDonald's misgivings stayed with him all evening. Even after he returned home. Doctor, who lived in the same house as MacDonald, noticed his troubled demeanor immediately and left him alone. And when Teacher showed up for dinner, he too noticed MacDonald's brooding, but he said nothing.

The house was crude, cruder than the average ape house. The room was plain with a rough fireplace. On the mantel were a few fresh flowers in an antique Coke bottle and a yellowing photograph of Martin Luther King in a corroded frame. Above the mantel hung a diploma from a black university, long since crumbled into ashes. There was also a photo of MacDonald's dead brother, the one human being who had helped Caesar. MacDonald had loved his brother—and he loved Caesar now—but there had been many moments since the ape uprising when he had longed for the old days.

MacDonald knew that slavery was wrong, he knew it instinctively, but if there had to be slaves and masters, he would much prefer to be a master. But then, every time he found himself thinking that way, he remembered a statement that Abraham Lincoln had made around 1851 or so, that if there was to be a difference between the black race and the white race, he, Abe Lincoln, would much prefer that the white race be the superior. The thought always made MacDonald smile. History had conveniently forgotten that statement of Lincoln's and remembered him primarily for the Emancipation Proclamation.

Caesar was a lot like Lincoln, too. He wanted apes and humans to be equal, but if there had to be slaves and masters, he would much prefer to be among the masters. The sentiment was universal, and because of it there were times when MacDonald's longing for the old days was especially fierce.

Like now, for instance.

The table was set for three. A single candle glowed in its center. There were rusty knives and forks and chipped enamel plates.

Teacher was putting two blankets over the window. "Apes have such an acute sense of smell," he was muttering.

MacDonald smiled and cautiously shut the outer door. He tested it and put a chair under the handle so no one could enter abruptly. Then he moved to the window and double-checked Teacher's precautions.

Satisfied, he opened the door to the other room and called, "Okay, Doctor, we're ready. Bring it in."

"I'm on my way," she answered. A moment later, she entered, carrying in one hand a flat black leather case and in the other a dish on which reposed "One roast bootleg rabbit!"

"Shhhh! Not so loud," said teacher.

Cautiously, she set down the dish and opened the leather case. She began extracting surgical instruments to carve the rabbit. The two men watched each cut intently.

She stopped and looked at both of them, amused. Her scalpel was poised in mid-stroke. "I'm being as fair as I can." She began filling their plates.

"I'm salivating like one of Pavlov's dogs." Teacher began stuffing his face.

MacDonald ate hungrily too. "Mmmf," he said

around a mouthful. "I just hope there's enough to go around. I'm famished."

She smiled at him as she sat down to eat. "Don't worry. There's plenty more." She cut herself a bite and ate it. "Not bad, if I do say so myself."

Both MacDonald and Teacher nodded but kept eating. These meals of meat were rare and always very secretive. It wasn't that rabbits were hard to catch—they weren't, they were very plentiful—it was just that the apes didn't allow the killing of any animal for any reason whatever. Not even for food. But rabbit tasted so good . . . Doctor had outdone herself; the rabbit had been seasoned just right. If MacDonald closed his eyes and pretended very hard, it almost tasted like chicken. *Almost* . . .

He snapped back to reality and reached for another forkful. The plate was almost empty. He sighed in disappointment and tried to make the last mouthful last. He hadn't remembered eating all that meat. But he had, he must have. The others' plates were empty, too. That was the trouble with rabbit—there was always enough to taste but never enough to fill. He laid the fork down regretfully. "I had hoped not to be marching on an empty stomach tomorrow, but that's an awful lot to demand of just one rabbit."

"Marching?" Teacher looked up. "Where?"

MacDonald lowered his voice. "Tomorrow, Virgil and I are taking Caesar to the city."

"The city? It must still be crawling with radioactivity."

"I know, but Caesar wants to go. *Has* to go."

"But there's nothing there! The city is dead."

"And so will you be," Doctor cut in sharply. "Unless you take a Geiger counter. Why are you going?"

"I told Caesar that there are tapes of his parents. He wants to see them."

Teacher dropped his fork on the plate with a clatter. "That's a stupid reason to risk your life."

"There's more to it than that," said MacDonald. "Something that I didn't tell Caesar, but something that I must find out. *We* must find out," he corrected.

"What is it?"

"I'm not sure. It's something that my brother told me, something that Caesar's parents said about the future. About ... the end of the world. We have to know what that is. I have to hear the tapes myself."

He thought back, to when he had been a boy, to a time when men had gone to the moon. And *beyond* ...

It had been an exciting time. The greatest mission of all had been when three men and a woman were launched into space to try to reach a nearby star. They had never returned, but the ship had come back, crashing off the California coast.

There had been three chimpanzees in it.

That had been the beginning of the end for the human race.

One of the chimpanzees had been killed, but two had survived, a male and a female named Cornelius and Zira. They had startled the world by their ability to speak, and they had revealed what had happened to Captain Taylor and the others, who had vanished on that fateful mission.

The ship had traveled not to another star but to the Earth's own future. Taylor had survived and discovered that the roles of apes and men were reversed. Apes were intelligent, and men were speechless animals, kept in cages. Discovering this, Taylor had fled into the wilderness to seek other men— *civilized* men.

Another spaceman had come after Taylor, and he too had vanished into the wilderness. Cornelius and Zira had discovered Taylor's spaceship, repaired it, and used it to travel back to Taylor's time.

They told what they knew, but the information was dangerous. Something they had said about the future, the *immediate* future, had frightened the government, and they had been sequestered. Zira had become pregnant, and to save the life of their baby, the two apes had escaped. But they had been discovered and killed, the baby chimpanzee with them.

Or, had the baby chimp been killed? A young chimp had been killed, but was it Cornelius' and Zira's? It would be years before the truth became known.

Half a generation later, the world was a different place. Cornelius and Zira had been forgotten—*almost*. One of their predictions had already come true: a plague had wiped out almost all of the dogs and cats in the world, and human beings had turned to apes and monkeys to take their place.

The government had become monolithic and totalitarian, fearful of its own future; it was a repressive and all-controlling state, and as such, it needed slaves. As the intelligence of chimpanzees and orangutans and the strength of gorillas became recognized, apes were given more and more work to do. Scientists worked to raise their intelligence level, and apes began to approach human levels of understanding. They became the slaves the government needed to keep its real slaves—the people—content.

And then the second prediction had come true: an ape had said "No" to his human masters. The ape was Caesar. He had been raised in secret by Armando, the owner of a traveling circus, who had brought him to the city to see and to fulfill his destiny. Armando had been killed, but Caesar had stayed free long enough to lead the apes in revolt against their human masters. He had been captured by Governor Breck and almost killed. But he had been rescued by MacDonald's brother. Caesar had led his people to freedom, and the world had plunged into war, and the cities had been flattened.

The few survivors, men and apes alike, returned to a simpler life. They lived in the forests, and the apes were the masters.

Now, today, nine years later, Caesar was going to go in search of his parents' image. And MacDonald, with him, was going to search for the truth—just what was it that Cornelius and Zira had said that had frightened the government so badly and turned it into a dictatorship? Was it really the end of the world? Two of their predictions had already come true. . . .

Just as Caesar had to know, so did MacDonald.

He came out of his reverie, realized that Doctor was looking at him. "Is this journey really necessary?" she asked.

He nodded slowly. "Yes. Yes, it is."

She accepted that. She got up out of her chair and came around to him. "Be careful, Mac," she said. "Please." She kissed him long and hard. "Come back."

He looked at her. "I have to know the truth."

She lowered herself to his lap and put her arms around his neck. "Mac," she whispered. "Life is more important than truth. If it costs you your life to find out the answer, what good will that do any of us?"

He couldn't answer her question, not the way she had phrased it. Instead, he kissed her and said, "I'll come back. And I'll come back *with* the answers."

And on the other side of Ape City, in a different house, an ape house, the same scene was being played between two apes.

"Caesar," Lisa was saying. "Don't go. Please don't go."

"Lisa, you remember your parents. I was too young when they died to remember mine."

Lisa stiffened. "I don't want to have to remember my husband. I want to love you now."

He took her outstretched hand against his cheek, then he took her into his arms and rubbed his muzzle against hers. "Lisa, Lisa, dear. My parents left me knowledge, I must go find it. Perhaps they left me the knowledge that I need to lead our people. Apes must be better than humans ever were. Apes must build a world of peace and justice, freedom and equality. My parents came from the future; they came from such a world. They came from a world of apes—it must have been a time of graciousness and plenty. I need to know how such a world was built; perhaps they brought me the answer. I must take the chance. I must be the kind of leader that my people need, and to do that, I must have the knowledge that a leader needs. Lisa, my love, my wife, you are important to me—you are the most important thing in my life. But I have a mission with our people. I cannot shirk that responsibility."

Lisa did not answer; she just lowered her eyes in sorrow.

Caesar kissed her. "I will take care, Lisa. I will."

Lisa looked up at her husband. Her eyes were moist. "Say good morning to Cornelius, then, but not good-by. I don't want him to know that I'm afraid."

Caesar smiled and nodded and rubbed her muzzle again in an affectionate chimpanzee kiss. Then he went into his son's bedroom. Cornelius slept on a raised pallet beside a table; on the table was his favorite pet, a caged squirrel.

Caesar laid an index finger lightly on Cornelius' forehead. Cornelius opened his eyes.

"Cornelius, I'm going on a journey."

Drowsily, the little chimp asked, "What will you bring me back?"

"What would you like?"

Cornelius pointed at his squirrel, "Some special nuts for Ricky. He's getting bigger."

Caesar smiled affectionately. "So are you." He touched his son's face. "One day you'll be as tall as a king."

THREE

The door was impressively stout. Caesar pounded on it loudly. MacDonald and Virgil stood beside him. Caesar pounded again.

"He's asleep," commented MacDonald.

"Not eternally, I hope," said Virgil.

Caesar pounded a third time. Impatiently.

From behind the door came an ancient voice. "Who knocks?"

"Caesar."

A tiny grille in the center of the door slid back, revealing the wizened face of a very old orangutan with red, rheumy eyes. His voice quavered as he asked, "And what does Caesar want?"

"Weapons."

The old orangutan peered harshly at the three of them. His name was Mandemus. "For what purpose?" he demanded.

Caesar nudged Virgil at that. Virgil stepped forward. "For self-protection in the pursuit of knowledge."

"Self-protection? Self-protection? Against whom or what?"

"We don't know," said Virgil.

"Hmp," said Mandemus. "Then what is the point of protecting yourself against a danger of which you have no knowledge while you pursue a knowledge you do not possess?"

At this, MacDonald rolled his eyes heavenward. "Oh, no!"

Mandemus continued implacably. "Is this knowledge for good or evil?"

Virgil answered without hesitation, "All knowledge is for good. Only the use to which you put it can be evil."

"The sun is rising," said Caesar. "I should like to settle this matter before it sets." He fidgeted impatiently.

Mandemus protested vehemently. "Caesar, you appointed me not only as the keeper of this armory but as the keeper of your own conscience. That is why I have asked six boring questions. And now I will ask a seventh before I decide whether to issue the weapons you think you require. What is the nature of the knowledge you cannot seek *without* weapons?"

MacDonald spoke then. "The knowledge of Earth's ultimate fate, recorded on tapes in the archives of the Forbidden City . . ."

Caesar added, ". . . which is contaminated, but may still be inhabited by humans."

Mandemus considered this. He chewed it over thoughtfully, pursing his lips and creasing his forehead in concentration. At last he decided. "Come in," he said. He released the bolt and pushed the heavy door aside for them to enter.

Inside, there were boxes of weapons and ammunition—all kinds, all sizes, salvaged from the great uprising. They were piled high in crates stacked against the walls—a mountain of madness and savagery that belied the peacefulness of Ape City. The room was lit by flickering lamps; they were upright wicks burning in small bowls of oil. MacDonald flinched when he realized. This armory was an explosion looking for a time to happen. But the apes would rather risk the destruction of their whole city than ever allow electricity to be wired into their homes. Electricity was too much a human thing; the apes identified it too much with the human cities and the time of their oppression. Worse, they associated it with the electrical cattle prods that had been used to condition them. But still . . . MacDonald shuddered, there must be a safer way to light the armory.

Caesar was moving around the cases, inspecting and frowning. Mandemus followed, waving his keys and gesturing. "Well, what is it Caesar needs?"

Caesar said without looking up, "Three machine guns."

Mandemus dropped his keys. "Three machine guns?"

"And ammunition," added MacDonald.

"For the removal of obstacles," put in Virgil.

Mandemus picked up his keys, muttering to himself. "Three machine guns. And ammunition. For the removal of obstacles." He looked from case to case, from pile to pile, from wall to wall, from dump to dump. I don't really hold with this. Searching for knowledge. Learning the future. I don't even want to know my own, which will be brief."

"And a Geiger counter," said Virgil.

Mandemus didn't hear him. He muttered on as he led them to the appropriate cases. "I mean if we knew for a fact that there was an afterlife and that the afterlife was bliss eternal, we'd all commit suicide in order to be able to enjoy it. But if there were an afterlife, what would be the purpose of this life? Except maybe to provide a place for us to earn the afterlife? But why must we earn an afterlife? Shouldn't we live this life for its own sake?"

Caesar, Virgil, and MacDonald ignored him. They had heard his incessant philosophizing before and had learned to ignore it. Mandemus babbled like a brook without saying anything. He was out of his time.

As Caesar and Virgil began unpacking the machine guns and ammunition, MacDonald thought of something else. "Pistols," he said.

Mandemus turned to him, eyeing him sharply. "For the removal of *smaller* obstacles?"

"This is a three-day journey," said Virgil. "With Caesar's permission, MacDonald may want to shoot, cook, and eat a rabbit."

MacDonald looked up sharply at this. Did Virgil know about his secret meals with Doctor and Teacher? Did Caesar know?

Mandemus snorted. "Who needs three pistols to shoot one rabbit?" He took a single Smith & Wesson out of a box and tossed it to MacDonald.

A pack of ammunition followed. "Here. Enjoy your meal."

The old orangutan bowed to Caesar then and ceremoniously ushered the trio out the great door, slamming it behind them. Mandemus didn't disapprove of weapons. He only disapproved of their use.

MacDonald commented wryly, "He may be old, but he has a mind like a razor."

Virgil agreed. "When I was a child, he was my teacher."

Caesar rumbled in his throat. "Enough. Let's get going." And the three moved off into the predawn darkness, not noticing that behind them the old orangutan was watching through the grille in his door. His face was skeptical, and his simian features were pursed in disappointment. Shaking his head sadly, he clanged the peephole shut and turned back to his armory.

The gorillas were the guardians of Ape City. It was the closest they could come to playing war. They built and manned their outposts and pretended they were important.

They didn't really care about Ape City, but they did care about being strong and fierce. And if the only way that they could be strong and fierce was to become the protectors of Ape City, then they would protect Ape City with all the fervor they could muster.

But for nine years there hadn't been a single threat against Ape City. None at all, aside from a few natural disasters. There had been an earth-

quake once, but it had been a little one; nothing
had been broken. There had been a couple of
floods, and once a landslide, which had ruined half
an orchard. But there had never been the threat
against Ape City that had required the gorillas to
stand up and fight.

No armies of men had ever come rolling across
the desert from the Forbidden City, threatening
with guns and fire and electric cattle prods. No
hordes of hungry savages had ever attacked, not
even a pack of marauding rebel apes. The gorillas
were ready for a fight, but there was nothing to
fight. The nine years would probably stretch into
ninety. Or nine hundred.

The result was boredom. The gorillas had long
since forgotten their original vigilance. They sat
around the fires of their outpost, grumbling and
picking at their fur, looking for fleas. They snorted
and grumbled and cursed, pretending that they
hated being out there in the cold night. But not
one of them wanted to go back to Ape City, where
the skinny little chimpanzees and the pale and effete orangutans were in charge. Out here, at least,
gorillas could be gorillas. Out here they didn't
have to bathe every week, as Caesar commanded
the other apes. Out here they didn't have to prac-
tice their reading and writing. Out here they could
play at war.

But they weren't even good at that.

As Caesar, MacDonald, and Virgil crept over the
ridge near the outpost, only one gorilla came alert.
He sniffed at the air curiously and grunted. He
poked one of his fellow guards. The other gorillas

ignored him. They didn't smell anything. Their senses had become blurred by disuse. Their vigil had been dulled by ennui.

Caesar, MacDonald, and Virgil passed undetected.

The sun rose to see them trudging across a region of sparse vegetation. The sky ahead went from black to deep blue, became bluer and bluer, then began getting pale, shading almost to white, then yellow and pink. Finally, a great ball of light showed its rim over the horizon and began climbing higher and higher to reveal itself as a blazing yellow orb. The sky around it was white with glare.

Their shadows stretched out behind them, then began shrinking as the sun climbed overhead. The morning began warming, and MacDonald shrugged out of his jacket. Later he loosened his shirt. The two apes too began to feel the heat but couldn't do anything about it.

The ground was covered with dry scrub grass and occasional cactus. There were large boulders sticking up out of the sand. Once they saw a snake slithering out to sun itself on one of them. Another time they saw a rabbit, but by the time MacDonald got his Smith & Wesson out and loaded, it had disappeared.

They stopped to rest at a water hole and chew on some of the dried fruits and nuts they had brought with them; Caesar sniffed at the water and wrinkled his nose in distaste. They used the water in their canteens instead. They waited out the hottest part of the day and then moved on.

Evening saw them still struggling over the

desert, the sun sinking behind them like a great red eye. The floor of the desert was sandy, and it was hard going, but they pushed on until it was too dark to see any more. Then and only then would Caesar let them stop for the night.

The stars were sharp, brilliant needlepoints of clarity, high and distant. The roof of the world was vast, filled with them. In the cold, dark night, surrounded by silence and stars, whipped by a cold breeze, MacDonald felt a chill in his bones. A chill and something more. He looked over at Caesar and Virgil. They were silent and stolid. He wondered if the two apes felt the same way when they looked at the incredible night sky. They were impassive.

What kind of emotions did apes have, anyway? They were more basic than humans—that was for sure. They were closer to nature. But, dammit, sometimes they seemed more rational than humans, more *removed* from life. And often they were impossible to decipher with their almost but not quite human expressions.

MacDonald fell asleep thinking about it. He dozed lightly. He kept waking up and falling asleep again. He tossed and turned and rolled around in his blanket. He slept fitfully on the hard cold ground, and his mind was troubled with images he couldn't identify, things that weren't distinct enough to be called dreams.

When he awoke, the two apes were already moving about, breaking up camp and preparing to hike on. MacDonald breakfasted lightly and unsatisfyingly on some dried fruits and joined them without comment. His head hurt from the uncomfortable, restless night.

Once more they trudged into the sunrise, Caesar in the lead, Virgil following eagerly, MacDonald beginning to show fatigue. The ground was rockier here, uneven and jagged. Several times he missed his footing and slipped. The apes were nimbler; they bounced from rock to rock.

It wasn't until he noticed the first twisted girders that MacDonald realized that it wasn't rocks he was stumbling over. It was shattered concrete.

He looked about him then, and with this new realization, saw that they had been walking through ruins for some time. As they moved up a low mound, he looked behind him and saw the shattered pattern of the city stretching out toward the distant horizon. He hadn't even noticed. It faded out into the desert so gradually one had to know it was there in order to see it.

They reached the top of the hill, and Caesar stopped in sudden shock. Virgil came up beside him, also startled. A moment later MacDonald joined them. His mouth fell open in horror. The three of them stared ahead in awe and amazement.

"There it is," said Caesar and then corrected himself. "Or was."

Virgil was solemn. "It looks like a storm at sea." he murmured. "But solidified."

"It was done by a bomb from an armory one thousand times the size of yours," said MacDonald.

"There must not have been anybody to keep its owner's conscience," remarked Virgil.

The three of them fell silent at that. They stood on the rise of ground and surveyed the nightmarish scene below.

As far as they could see, stretching to the distant horizon, the landscape was a jumbled ruin. It was the total desolation of one of man's great cities, and it lay in a shambles of twisted and melted girders and concrete, shattered automobiles, fallen buildings, and ruined highways. The destruction was total. The city was massive, silent, and utterly dead. A monument to madness. A tribute to the game of war. The ultimate playground for generals. And gorillas.

The horrifying part of the scene was that it was also beautiful. There was a savage kind of color splashed across the land—reds and yellows and browns, streaked with blacks and whites in stark patterns. The texture of the desolation was brutally attractive, almost *lovely* in its roughness. It was too horrible to be real. And yet it was.

MacDonald's voice was shaky. "London, Rome, Athens, Rio, Moscow, Tokyo, Peking . . ."

Virgil's voice was firmer. "And Hell . . ."

But Caesar was firmest. "That's where we're going." He moved resolutely forward. The other two exchanged a glance and followed him down the hill and into the worst of the ruins.

They clambered over surfaces that had been liquid for one brief but endless moment and then had become solid again. The city had not been blown apart—it had been melted, like a candle left out in the sun, but a sun a million times hotter and a million times closer.

Glass, masonry, steel—all had been dissolved by the incredible temperature at the center of the bomb. Everything seemed to have a smooth surface; everything seemed fused together. The buildings and structures had crumpled and flowed into one another; the city was a single piece of undifferentiated slag, a mountain of glass with cars, buses, and other objects too melted to identify, sticking out of it, a glacier of savagery and hatred.

MacDonald was thoroughly shaken by the horror around him. His eyes were moist, but his face was expressionless with horror. Even the two apes were ashen at the sight of so much destruction.

The man's mind churned with thoughts; half-remembered phrases came unbidden to him, descriptions out of Dante, Kafka, and Sade. Hell was too pale a term to describe what they were passing through.

"My God," he murmured. "My God. How could they have let this happen?" But there was no answer, not from the apes. Not from anyone else.

Caesar pointed toward a structure that seemed to be an underground entrance. "There," he said. "Is that it?"

MacDonald peered, abruptly surprised out of his reverie. He nodded.

Virgil sniffed and took out the Geiger counter. He switched it on; it clattered, but not too loudly. He pursed his lips and frowned as he studied the meter on the device. "We are at best brave and at worst mad to be here. This background radiation alone will give us at least three hundred roentgens an hour."

"Meaning?" Caesar looked at him.

"That if we're not out of here within two hours, we shall become . . . inmates."

"Hmf," said Caesar. "Then we had better hurry." He moved toward the entrance impatiently, MacDonald and Virgil hurrying to keep up.

MacDonald climbed down past the rubble first, hoping to identify the tunnel. He sniffed the air as he moved. It smelled stale and musty; the tunnel was old and unused.

He didn't recognize it at first, though. He stopped at an intersection and stood there frowning in puzzlement. He lit a torch and waved it back and forth, searching for some familiar or identifying mark, until finally Caesar and Virgil climbed impatiently down themselves. Caesar was brusque. "You've got your bearings?"

"I think so, yes. This is . . . was . . . Eleventh Avenue. Ape Management was one block east of here; the Archives Section two blocks west, at the corner of Breck Street and Ackerman. We want department 4SJ."

"Get us there—quickly," ordered Caesar. "Let's go."

MacDonald nodded and led them down one of the corridors toward a lower level.

"I was here so often," whispered MacDonald, half to himself. "When the city was alive."

"And existing on *our* labor," snorted Caesar.

MacDonald looked at him sharply. "They paid, Caesar. They all paid."

They groped their way along the dimly lit passage. It was damp and full of debris. The two apes wrinkled their noses in distaste, but they padded on through the rubble. The Geiger counter clicked in counterpoint.

"Dead," muttered MacDonald. "Dead . . . dead . . . all of them dead."

But he was wrong. Very wrong.

The city was very much alive. Perhaps not on the scale it had been nine years before, but still alive enough to be dangerous.

Down, down, farther down, buried in the bowels, deep enough even to have withstood the inferno that had raged above and leveled the rest of the city, were layer upon layer of levels, shielded by concrete and girders—the secret nerve center of the city's control when it was alive and the center of its activity even in "death."

The rooms and corridors were a shambles, largely destroyed, crumbling, peeling, scarred, and burned.

So were the people. Crumbling, peeling, scarred, and burned. Destroyed by the radiation around them.

Their leader was Kolp. He was fat and sallow and had watery eyes. He had been lieutenant to Governor Breck, the man who had captured and tried to kill Caesar. He was changed now, his face ravaged by time and radiation. His beard was uneven across the scars. His hands were sometimes palsied, his movements rough and painful, and his voice harsh and grating. His eyes moved constantly, searching back and forth, darting quickly from corner to corner, fearful of sudden noises and unseen assassins. He sat before a shabby, dust-covered console and manipulated its useless dials.

He was not alone. Sitting at another console was a woman named Alma. Once she had been beautiful. She still was, despite the damaging radiation. But her eyes were glazed with madness. Unable to cope with the terrible collapse of her world and everything in it, she had fled into insanity. Only occasionally did she test the waters of rationality, and each time, finding them still too fearful, she retreated once more into fantasy. It was the only response that protected her from pain and from the acceptance of death. Kolp protected her too. Kolp was strong, and she needed someone strong . . .

Kolp liked to pretend that the city was still alive; it pleased him. He made Alma play the game too—only to Alma it was no longer a game. Alma believed it because Kolp had taught her to. Yet, sometimes . . . sometimes her brow wrinkled in puzzlement. If the city was still alive, why weren't there more people? Sometimes she questioned the thought and followed it, but she was always careful not to follow it too far. That way lay rationality and the madness that the rational world had become.

"Alma," Kolp said suddenly. "Get me the Chamber of Commerce."

This was one of those moments for Alma. How to solve it? Ah . . . "There's still a chamber. Mr. Kolp. But no commerce."

"I know that," he growled irritably. "I just want to talk to somebody. Anybody. Isn't there a doorman or something?"

Alma knew how to play the game. She smiled sweetly in her madness. "There's no door. You know that too."

Kolp made a noise deep in his throat. Sometimes Alma could be annoying. Dreadfully so.

"If the bomb hadn't killed the old governor," he muttered, "then boredom certainly would have. This is a ghost city. There aren't enough people to lead. There's nothing left but bones. I want to put flesh on them."

"Radioactive flesh?" Alma knew what that meant. They all had taken drugs that made it possible for them to survive the intense radiation of the ruins. The drugs worked to speed up the process of regeneration, helped the ravaged flesh repair itself; the one drawback was that the genetic information was damaged. The cells divided and multiplied but not according to the body's original plan. The drugs kept them alive; they didn't keep them beautiful.

Kolp didn't respond to Alma's remark; she babbled like that all the time.

"We're all radiated," she was saying. "But at least we're active." Alma was playing word games again.

Kolp decided to cut her off. "Get me the chief of . . ."

But suddenly Alma said, "Mr. Kolp!" Her voice was frightened, like a child's.

"Huh?" He turned to look at her.

She was pointing at her console. A tiny red light was flashing on it. "Look."

He advanced slowly. The two peered curiously at

the insistent signal. "What is it?" He searched his memory.

"It's a signal. It's an alert." Old routines came flashing to memory.

"There's somebody in the tunnels?"

She touched the console in wonderment, then flicked switches to isolate the location. "F-6," she said.

"Alert Méndez," snapped Kolp. "No, I'll do it." He hurried out of the rubble-strewn command center, followed by a nervous Alma. She ran in little half-steps after him, she didn't want to be left alone now—not at a time like this when something new was threatening her lack of rationality.

Kolp moved quickly through his underground world. His palsy vanished in his excitement, although his movements were still jerky. He crossed a balcony overlooking a work area where radiation-ravaged men and women were working at various tasks.

Some of the mutated men were trying to repair a fleet of lumbering gray military vehicles. Others were polishing and oiling weapons, putting them in readiness for what unknown battles they couldn't guess. The women were collecting huge mounds of canned food and clothing; there were daily search parties scavenging throughout the city. The life of the underground levels was the life of the pack rat and the scavenger. Nothing was wasted, this was a society of ragpickers and tramps. They moved like zombies, with an almost mechanical efficiency, the same kind of nonvolitional activity one might associate with a beehive or an ant hill.

This huge underground vault was a partially collapsed public air raid shelter. Now it had become one of the collection centers for the salvaged remains of the city's wealth in goods.

Overlooking the far end of the vault was another control center. This one was more extensive than the one that Kolp had made his headquarters. Méndez, Kolp's chief lieutenant, used it for coordinating the collection and distribution of supplies. He too was marred by radiation, as were all the mutants living in the levels below the ruins. He was devoted to Kolp, slavishly so; he was happy to play at war, but even happier that there was no enemy to fight.

"Méndez!" barked Kolp, striding up to him in his control center. "Someone's breached the warning signal at entry point F-6."

Méndez was calm. "Must be one of our scavengers."

"No. That entry's locked. We've never used it."

Méndez scratched his cheek thoughtfully. "The warning is still operational?"

Alma nodded eagerly.

"So it can't be one of us," insisted Kolp. "It must be someone else. I want the security forces alerted."

"Well," said Méndez doubtfully. "I don't know. We ought to check it first. Sir," he added.

"Well, then do so!" snapped Kolp. "And quickly!"

Méndez led them to a set of consoles; here was a bank of still functioning television screens. He leaned across the control panel and began switching them on. One after the other, the monitors blinked alive, flickering with images of the underground corridors and of the blasted city above.

"Come on," said Méndez impatiently.

Méndez began stabbing buttons. The images on the screens began to flicker and change with dizzying rapidity. Then suddenly, abruptly, there was a startlingly close shot of a fierce-looking chimpanzee, a curious orangutan, and a nervous black man, moving cautiously through a dimly lit passage. The image flickered on to another. Kolp almost screamed.

"No! There! Go back!"

Méndez reversed the scan. The image of the three reappeared on the soundless monitor.

"My God!" gasped Kolp.

"What is it?" asked Alma. Méndez looked at him sharply. Kolp's face was ashen. "It's Caesar!"

"Caesar?"

"That damned chimpanzee! He's come back to reconquer the city!"

"Doesn't he know that the bombs did that?" Méndez' voice was edged with bitterness.

"He must know now . . ." They watched as the two apes and the man moved into a brighter section of corridor.

"It's cleaner here," Virgil was saying. He was referring to the radiation count. He moved slowly ahead of Caesar and MacDonald, watching his meter carefully.

"Could anything live here?" asked Caesar. "I mean after so long?"

Virgil was matter of fact in his answer. "Oh, yes. But I don't think it would be much of a life." The three moved on slowly, carefully. MacDonald had his machine gun loaded and ready; its muzzle swung back and forth, searching for targets.

Watching them on the monitors, Kolp wished the microphones were still working. He would have given anything to know what they were talking about.

"Who are the others?" asked Alma.

Kolp said angrily, "The black man is the brother of Breck's personal assistant, the one who helped Caesar escape. It figures—it must run in the blood. Damned traitors! Betrayers of the human race! His name is MacDonald; he used to supervise the general archives. Now he's helping apes!" He spat the words. After a moment he added, "I don't know who the orangutan is."

Caesar, Virgil, and MacDonald climbed over a sudden pile of rubble where a wall had collapsed, then turned a corner. They stopped in shock. Ahead of them in the tunnel, in the midst of all the dirt and tumbled concrete, were fragments of newspapers, rotting briefcases, bits of old clothing, and bones. Lots of bones. A skull grinned hollowly at them.

"This isn't a city," said Caesar. "It's a catacomb." He pushed forward, anyway, taking care to step around the rotting skeletons. Virgil followed. The two apes kept their eyes averted. MacDonald didn't—he had realized something that they had missed. Not all of the skeletons were whole. Some of the bones were scattered about. And some of them looked *gnawed*.

He raised his gun and moved closer to Caesar,

without explaining why. Maybe there was nothing alive down here now, but there had been at one time.

In the control center, Méndez switched to another camera to keep them in view.

"There are only three of them," he said.

"There must be more," said Alma. "I wonder how many?"

Kolp rubbed his hands together slowly. "That's a question we'll get answered when we get *them*."

On the screen they saw that the three explorers had reached a narrow, short, dark tunnel. The two apes lit their torches and poked them carefully into the gloom. They moved cautiously forward, sniffing and listening. The air smelled of death, tasted of foulness and decay. Somewhere something was whirring softly.

The passage was jammed with debris and rubble. There were places where it was piled so high that it brought them up close to the ceiling. They had to stoop to get through. As they moved through the tunnel, they could see that someone had once tried to live in one of its nooks. There were blankets, empty food tins, and a forlorn photo in a warped frame.

Suddenly, startlingly, a figure leaped up before them, an ugly, misshapen silhouette. MacDonald tensed. He fumbled with his tommy gun, but before he could fire, the figure scurried off. He dropped his torch and grabbed the gun with both hands, but whoever or whatever it was had disappeared down a side corridor. Its footsteps echoed loudly and hung in the air for a long moment.

The two apes and the man exchanged a startled glance. MacDonald forced himself to relax. He picked up his torch again and relit it from Virgil's. He forced himself to take a deep breath, then another. And then he tensed again; he frowned and moved toward a wall, holding his torch close to it, his machine gun ready in his other hand.

Written on the wall, dimmed by nine years of dust, dirt, and decay, were the words: "CONTROL CENTRAL—ARCHIVES SECTION."

"This is the place," said MacDonald quietly. He gestured with the torch. "In there." The light flickered to illuminate a twisted door and a crumbled room beyond. They began to clamber over the rubble and twisted metal, squeezing their way into the archives room.

Kolp finally turned away from the monitor screens. He picked up a microphone and, obviously enjoying himself, announced: "All security forces alert! Check out all sections in areas M-5, R-7, and R-8. Apprehend three strangers—one human and two apes." Below him, on the floor of the great vault, the workers hesitated; they turned toward him curiously and stared up at the control center. Then, as the meaning of his words sank in, the crowd moaned with an odd wail of anticipation and foreboding, a long drawn out "Aaaah." A mutter of fear.

"But use caution!" urged Kolp. "I repeat, use caution! If they resist, you may shoot."

Beside him, Méndez winced.

Kolp added, "But shoot only to maim. We want them alive for interrogation."

The crowd began to move then; it began to surge and flow in new directions. Like a great, amorphous, gray and white mass, the grotesque figures rolled restlessly through the cavern, sorting themselves into action, jerky and unsure. Section leaders began calling directions, but the movement was spastic.

Gradually the routines and the drills took hold. The men began breaking out the savage tools of destruction. Hands reached for weapons, pulled them off racks on the wall. Other hands broke open cases, pulled out ammunition. The smell of excitement—and fear—rose in the air. The rifles were passed eagerly from hand to hand; the bolts were slid back and checked in their action. Cartridges were dropped into chambers. Bodies began to move toward the tunnels. They poured into the corridors, Kolp's last speech still resounding through the cavern. Over and over, the words "Caution, caution!" rang along the walls.

In the Archives Section, Caesar, MacDonald, and Virgil were still stumbling over chunks of fallen concrete. Virgil paused for a moment as his Geiger counter clacked a little louder and quicker. He moved on, and the noise subsided.

As it did, he cocked his head curiously. There was *another* noise, a whirring sound. He stopped and looked around. He sniffed the air, his simian nostrils flaring. He blinked and held his torch aloft—and froze as he caught sight of the TV camera mounted high on the wall. It turned slowly this way and that, still scanning what had once been an entrance. The whirring came from its motor. It swung toward them and stopped. Virgil caught his breath.

He touched Caesar, pointing. "Look . . ."

Both MacDonald and Caesar stared at the camera. It stared impassively back at them.

MacDonald laughed at Virgil's fear. "It's been there for years. Breck used to have all the corridors equipped with cameras." He added wryly, "To forestall ape conspiracies, as I remember."

"No, no . . . it . . . was moving."

"What?"

"Are you sure?" asked Caesar.

Virgil nodded, never taking his eyes off the camera.

MacDonald licked his lips. His mouth was suddenly dry. He swallowed and took a step sideways. The camera moved slightly to follow him, its motor whirring softly.

"He's . . . right. Virgil's right!"

Virgil lifted his gun and held the trigger down for one long, angry moment. A burst of machine gun fire tore the camera off the ceiling. Pieces of it scattered across the room, ricocheted off the walls. Only a few dangling wires remained.

He stood there with his machine gun smoking. Caesar and MacDonald stared at him, hardly believing what he had done.

"Whoever or whatever is down here . . ." began Caesar.

". . . already knows that we're here too," finished Virgil.

"That camera was supposed to make automatic sweeps—it wasn't," said MacDonald. "It was being manually controlled."

"We've got to get out of here," said Virgil.

"Not until we find those tapes," snapped Caesar. "Come on." He scrambled forward. MacDonald and Virgil followed.

FOUR

"Those apes!" cried Kolp. "I'll get them for that!" He slammed his fist against the TV monitor. The screen remained blank. "They must have shot the whole camera off."

"If we shoot them," said Méndez, "we break years of peace."

Kolp misunderstood him. "I know," he said. "It's been boring, hasn't it?"

Méndez didn't answer. Frowning to himself, he began switching the monitor screens to show the views from other TV cameras. He couldn't pick up the intruders, though. "They've gone all the way into the Archives Section."

"Huh?" Kolp looked at him. "Archives? What do they want there?"

"It must be important, whatever it is."

"Blueprints," muttered Kolp. "Plans for the underground city. That's what they want. They must be planning to attack us again. That's what it is, I'll bet! I'm sure of it!" His expression grew cunning. And savage. "Well, we'll get them. Yes, we will. We'll get them."

In the Archives Section, MacDonald, Caesar, and Virgil were already ripping open cartons, pulling apart crumbling file cabinets, and pawing through piles of tape canisters.

The two apes were trying to be systematic; they were picking up one tape canister at a time and reading its label, frowning darkly and moving their lips, then carefully discarding it as they decided it was not the one they were looking for and moving on to the next.

MacDonald was less careful. He was in a hurry. He knew what he was looking for and approximately where it should be. He shuffled through the files and tapes with barely controlled fury. Impatience and a need to get out of there quickly drove him to this impetuosity. "It'll be a tape, a big, round canister," he said. But he was only repeating himself. He had briefed the two apes many times during their journey across the desert. They all knew what they were looking for and where it should have been stored.

Should have been. But wasn't. The room had collapsed long ago. Filing cabinets had toppled over, their contents scattered. Someone had been in here, too; whoever it was hadn't shown much regard for the files. Papers and tapes were scattered haphazardly.

The filing cabinets and shelves were of no help, either. The tape wasn't there. It would have to be one of the ones buried in the rubble on the floor. The three of them began digging through the piles of papers and tapes and films. They had to examine them all, each one individually. Abruptly, Virgil straightened. He held a large tape canister in his hand. "MacDonald," he said. "Is this it?" He read aloud from the label, " 'Proceedings of the Presidential Commission on Alien Visitors.' "

Caesar and MacDonald joined him and looked over his shoulder. "I think . . ." said MacDonald. "Yes, that must be it."

"Good," said Caesar. "Let's play it."

MacDonald started to say something, then closed his mouth. He wanted to leave, but Caesar was right—the tape had to be played. There were no videotape players in Ape City. Quickly, he threaded the tape into a machine, all the while muttering, "Oh, please let it work." He pressed the switch. The tape reels began turning slowly; the tape slid past the playback head. "Thank you," MacDonald whispered to no one in particular.

Caesar seated himself very close to the monitor and waited impatiently. He fidgeted. MacDonald touched the fast-forward button and moved to a later point on the tape. Abruptly the screen came alive with the image of a female chimpanzee, an oddly beautiful face, somehow both kind and alien.

"Is that her?" whispered Caesar hoarsely, shifting in his seat to look at MacDonald. "Is that her?" He didn't wait for an answer. He pressed his face close to the screen and sniffed. "Mother . . ." he said. "Mother?" The word felt curious in his mouth.

"Is there sound?" prompted Virgil.

"Oh . . ." said MacDonald. He touched another

control. Abruptly, Zira's voice came from the speaker: "It wasn't *our* war. It was the gorillas' war. Chimpanzees are pacifists. We stayed behind. We never saw the enemy."

"Why does her voice sound so thick?" asked Virgil.

"They got her drunk; it was the only way they could get her to talk."

"Mother . . ." whispered Caesar. His face was rapt.

Another voice on the tape, a human voice, asked, "But which side won?"

Zira's voice replied flatly, "Neither."

Virgil and MacDonald exchanged a worried glance. Caesar didn't react; he was too absorbed in the flickering images of his mother. The screen was flashing through a series of color stills. Zira was lovely; her eyes were bright, large and brown and alive with warmth. Most of the pictures showed her smiling; her face creased easily into a smile. Zira had been a true madonna.

The voice on the tape continued, "How do you know if you weren't there?"

"When we were in space . . ." said Zira, "we saw a bright white, blinding light. We saw the rim of the Earth melt. Then there was a . . . tornado in the sky."

After a pause, the human voice asked, "Zira, was there a date meter in the spaceship?"

"Mmm."

"What year did it register after Earth's destruction?"

Zira's speech was blurred, but the words were still understandable. "Thirty-nine fifty."

The monitor screen went white.

Caesar snarled bitterly and looked up at Virgil. "And you talk to your pupils about eternity!"

The screen flickered, and another image appeared, this one a male chimpanzee. Caesar's father, Cornelius. Caesar reached out and touched the image's cheek. "Father ..." He felt odd saying this word. And somehow hollow.

The same human interrogator was asking, "How did apes first acquire the power of speech?"

Cornelius' voice—oddly like Caesar's—came from the speaker. "They learned to *refuse*. At first they barked their refusal. And then on a historic day, commemorated by my species and fully documented in the secret scrolls, there came an ape who didn't bark. He articulated. He spoke a word which had been spoken to him, times without number, by humans. He said 'No.'"

The screen flickered and went black; the tape had run out. The end of it flapped around the takeup reel. Absent-mindedly MacDonald stopped it. He switched off the machine and removed the tape. "Since your father was right," he said, "we must assume that your mother was right about the year of the world's destruction."

"No wonder the governor was so anxious to have me killed."

"Not just the governor. All mankind thirsted for your blood and wanted your birth aborted. In the year 3950, apes will destroy the Earth."

Virgil interjected quickly, "Not apes. Gorillas. But that's only *one* possible future."

They both looked at him. "How can there be more than one?" asked Caesar.

"Time has an infinite number of possibilities," said Virgil. "It must have. We can change the present, can't we? We must be able to change the future. There must be a way."

Caesar stood up. "Yes," he agreed. "There must be. Because if there isn't ... then there is no point in going on. No point in planning and building and learning. No point in justice. There's no point in building a better world if you know it has no chance of survival."

"That's precisely why we *have* to change the future," said Virgil. "And the way to do it is by making a world where wars are impossible. If we can do that, then there will be no final war. We must continue to have hope!"

Caesar looked at him. "Yes, Virgil, you're right. As usual." He smiled. "There's much that we have to change. Let's get started. Let's go." He headed for the door.

As the three squeezed out of the Archive Section, they heard a noise. Virgil cocked his head, then Caesar. MacDonald's ears were not as keen, but he caught it, too. Shouts. And the sound of running feet. A lot of them.

"This way!" he cried, and pointed. "Come on!" They raced down a lateral corridor.

A corridor scanned by a TV camera.

"There they are again!" cried Alma, pointing to

the TV monitors. Kolp and Méndez crowded close to watch the progress of Caesar and his friends.

Kolp grabbed a microphone. "Area Fourteen Security! They're running away! Stop them! They're going down corridor 11-M."

From a console speaker, a voice replied, "We're at the junction of corridor 11-M and 44-W. Subjects will have to pass us to escape!"

"Stop them! Do you hear? Bring them to me!"

"Yes, sir."

Caesar, Virgil, and MacDonald were just approaching that junction. Caesar stopped abruptly and sniffed. He paused, sniffed again, turning his head this way and that. His eyes flicked from side to side. Virgil did the same. MacDonald scuffed to a stop and stared at them. "What's holding you up? We have to get out of here!"

Virgil's Geiger counter clacked louder. He aimed it forward and its incessant clatter increased even more.

Caesar said, "Do you smell them, Virgil?"

"Yes . . . they're humans . . . but not like MacDonald."

Caesar moved ahead carefully, signaling for the others to do the same. He kept his head cocked, listening, alert, ready for trouble. He moved slowly into the junction of the passageways.

And screaming, hideous figures jumped on him from the side corridors. They were dressed in grubby black uniforms and heavy goggles.

MacDonald leveled his gun, but held his fire—they were too close to Caesar. The chimpanzee snarled, whirled around, biting and snapping, suddenly breaking free of the grabbing hands. Seeing MacDonald and Virgil with their guns ready, he hollered, "Shoot! Now!" He leapt clear and began firing his own gun.

MacDonald and Virgil blasted away at the mutants. Backing away as they fired, they followed Caesar into a darkened corridor, suddenly turning and running. Their assailants, confused and shocked, came scrabbling after them.

Watching his screens, Kolp was enraged. "They got past! They got past! All right—then shoot them on sight. Never mind about bringing them here! Just *get them!*"

His voice reached a hysterical pitch. His face was contorted with rage. Méndez and Alma exchanged concerned glances.

"Get them!" Kolp was shouting. "Get them! Get them! Kill them! Kill them! Kill them!"

The deformed creatures slogged up the corridor after the trio of intruders. Kolp's words blasted in their ears—from walkie-talkies and loudspeakers, from remote command posts and individual ear pieces. "Get them! Kill them! Kill them!"

The chimpanzee, the orangutan, and the man struggled up the corridor, exhausted by their run-in with the mutants. They approached another junction.

There was a sharp flash and an explosion of sound *ahead* of them, then a rapid staccato. They were being shot at. MacDonald felt something thump into his side, blossoming into a rivet of molten pain—he clutched at his wound, almost toppled, then threw himself backward against the wall. The two apes dropped backward, too. Seeing that MacDonald had been hit, Virgil crawled to him. Bullets ricocheted around them. "We've got to get out of here!" gasped the man.

Virgil gently pulled MacDonald's hands away from his side and peered carefully at the wound. "It appears to be only a crease in the epidermis," he remarked, then asked, "Is there another way out of here?"

MacDonald pointed back down the way they had come.

"I'll find out," said Caesar. "Stay here, but be ready to move ... fast!" He strode off down the corridor, away from the mutant-controlled junction. As he moved, in his funny hunchbacked way, he watched for an alternate exit from the maze of underground passages. He cast his gaze from side to side.

There it was! A large door that they had passed on their way up, leading to a closed-off side corridor. He pushed at it—it gave a little bit, then stopped. He pushed harder—it gave a little more. Caesar anchored his feet against the rubble and pushed with all his strength. If he could get it open just enough for them to squeeze through ...

Abruptly the door stuck. It would open no farther. Well, that would just have to do. Caesar squeezed halfway through and looked. There was an exit light very far ahead, a long way off down the tunnel. Yes, this was a way out!

He pulled back and yelled up to Virgil and MacDonald, "I've found it! Come on!"

MacDonald lurched to his feet, Virgil helping

him. The two came running down the corridor. They squeezed painfully through the door, first Caesar, then MacDonald—the apes helping him— then Virgil, following. "Hurry!" he yelped. "Hurry!" There were mutants racing toward him from both ends of the tunnel. Somewhere a voice, a strangely reverberating voice, was yelling, "Kill them! Kill them! Kill them!"

Virgil jumped through after MacDonald, he was the smallest of the three, and together they ran toward the distant exit light. MacDonald moved slowest because of his wound; the two apes were almost dragging him. Behind them they could hear the sound of running boots.

There was a junction of corridors up ahead. "Wait!" cried Caesar, skidding to a stop. He sniffed the air, paused to listen. Virgil, too.

The orangutan pointed down one of the side corridors, "They're coming from down there!"

"No!" said MacDonald, pointing down the other. "From there!"

"You're both right!" snapped Caesar. "From everywhere!" Behind them, more mutants were pouring into the corridor.

"Ahead!" cried the chimp, and they ran on. They came to the light Caesar had seen; it marked a T-shaped junction. They dashed to the left, then turned the first corner to the right.

Suddenly, they were running straight into a pack of mutants, who were charging down on them. Virgil started firing his tommy gun first, then Caesar. Even MacDonald managed to get off a few quick bursts, the pain in his side was excruciating.

The mutants screamed and tried to retreat, but those in back kept coming. They bunched up in the corridor. And died as the bullets splattered into them.

They screamed. They tried to run. They scrabbled at the walls. They fought to get away from the apes' blasting weapons. They clambered over one another. And died.

The survivors broke and ran.

The two apes and the man came charging after them, still firing. The grotesque figures ducked into side corridors and disappeared, vanished down junctions or into holes in the walls—anything to escape the savagery following them, hacking at their backs.

"There's the exit!" gasped MacDonald. "Up ahead. Keep going."

The end of the tunnel was lit by a stronger and brighter light. It streamed down into the gloomy darkness like a yellow beacon. They headed eagerly for it. Faster and faster. There were mutants pounding at their backs.

And then they were out. In the ruins. Running down a deserted city street. Disappearing into the melted buildings.

Kolp was livid. His expression was twisted with anger and frustration. He confronted the captain of Security. He raged at him. He bellowed like a wounded bull. He strode and waddled around the man and berated him. He vented his fury on the poor hapless captain, as if he were one of the apes himself.

"You had a *hundred* armed men!" cried Kolp. "You know these corridors down to the last nut and bolt. Yet they escaped! They *escaped!* You cretinous troglodyte! You filthy, slime-wallowing, trash-eating son of a worm! *You let them escape!*"

The captain of Security was as badly scarred as the rest of the men. He looked at Kolp and the rest of the council nervously. "They were fast, sir. And smart—the chimp surprised us, Governor. He found another exit."

"But he's only an animal!" shouted Kolp. "Nothing but an animal!"

"No, Governor," said Méndez. "He's more than an animal. He can speak. So can they all."

Kolp was scornful, "Hah! It takes more than the ability of speech to make a creature human!" He scowled, his scarred cheeks creased with pain.

"Speech makes them intelligent," insisted Méndez. "It gives them the power to manipulate ideas. Intelligence may not make them human, but it might make them humane. Perhaps they came in peace."

"They were armed!"

"Maybe only for their self-protection."

"You were looking at the same monitors I was, Méndez," snapped Kolp. "Did that look like self-protection to you?"

"Yes, it did. They only fired back after they were fired on."

"You're soft on apes, Méndez," Kolp snarled. "And stupid! They shot out one of our cameras. That's an act of war! And you saw how they hunted down our men and shot them in the back! Those apes are savages!"

"I still say we ought to let them return in peace."

"So they can raid us again? And again?" And then Kolp stopped. "Return?" he asked. "To where?"

"To wherever they came from. They must have a settlement somewhere."

"Yes," agreed the governor, stroking his uneven beard. "Yes . . . They must have a place some-where—but where? Where *do* they live? We ought to know," he muttered to himself. "They might try to come back. Now that they know we're still alive, they might try to exterminate the rest of us."

"They came with few provisions," chimed Alma. "They can't live too far away."

"Which way did they head?" Kolp asked.

The captain of Security was relieved that Kolp was no longer raging at him. "They headed north-west, Governor," he said quickly.

"Ahh, yes. Good. Organize scout parties. Collect all the equipment that will still work. Follow them. Find their hideout."

"Yes, sir. Right away, sir!" The captain saluted and wheeling about on one heel, hurried out.

Méndez looked at Kolp. "Why?" he asked.

Kolp grinned at him. "So that *we* can exterminate *them*." He rubbed his hands together and giggled. "Won't that be fun?"

FIVE

Aldo stood on the ridge and peered out into the desert. Somewhere out there lay the Forbidden City. Someday, someday ... He sniffed the air and curled his lip. Someday he would lead an army out there!

Behind him, the other gorillas sat at a small, almost burned-out fire, muttering and grunting, picking their fleas and cracking them.

Abruptly, Aldo stiffened. "Quiet," he barked to his troops.

Eyes narrowing, he looked out into the desert. Was there something out there? Other gorillas moved up to look, too. They sniffed at the wind.

Far out, almost lost in the sparsely vegetated terrain, were three figures, too distant to be identified. His hackles rose, and he growled deep in his throat. Were they men or apes? "Look ... there!" he pointed. The other gorillas looked, then reacted. They snorted, they snuffled, they flared their nostrils and fidgeted; they bounced up and down, they grunted, they made noises. They squinted and sniffed and became excited. They stamped their feet and pounded the ground.

"Quiet!" snapped Aldo again. His eyes narrowed to slits. The short, fat one must be an orangutan; yes, he could tell by the way the paunchy little thing waddled. The one on the other side, the one who was limping, was definitely a man. Aldo sneered. The third figure was walking like an ape. Too skinny to be a gorilla. Must be a chimp. Hmf. What were they doing out in the desert, anyway? The desert and the city were forbidden.

Aldo growled orders to his troops. They backed down off the ridge, out of sight.

As Caesar, Virgil, and MacDonald came climbing up the hill, the gorillas came charging down the slope and flung themselves on the trio.

"Hey, what . . . ?" cried Virgil, as he disappeared under the thundering black bodies. They went tumbling down over the rocks.

There was the flash of a drawn sword.

Caesar was yelling, "Stop . . . it's us . . . it's Caesar!"

"Caesar?" Aldo frowned. "Stop," he called. "Stop." He said it without urgency, only curiosity. "Caesar?" The scuffling muttered off into embarrassed silence. The two apes and the man stood up, brushing off the dirt.

"That's some welcome," said MacDonald wryly. "We should have stayed in the city. Definitely."

"I imagine Aldo was hoping we'd stay there *in*-definitely," remarked Virgil.

Aldo came down the slope toward them. "Why

were you there? To visit the city is forbidden." His manner was grim.

Caesar was just as cold. "I know. *I* forbade it."

"Then why . . . ?" Aldo frowned in puzzlement. This did not make sense to him.

"Aldo," said Virgil. "If a king forbids his subjects to wear a crown, that doesn't mean he can't wear one himself. Caesar is Caesar. He went to the city for a purpose."

"What purpose?" Aldo was suspicious.

"I went looking for my past, but I found our future."

"Huh? Explain." The big gorilla was aggressively insistent.

Caesar snarled irritably. "You wouldn't understand." He started to shove past Aldo.

But Aldo stopped him. He raised his sword and pointed it directly at Caesar's heart. "Aldo will make the future—with this."

"No," Caesar shook his head. "With that, Aldo will find himself in the past."

MacDonald smothered a smile, but Virgil laughed out loud. The trio moved up the hill and on toward Ape City.

The gorillas snorted in contempt and moved back toward their outpost. Not a single one noticed the three mutant scouts who had been tracking Caesar all the way from the city. The mutants began moving away from the outpost, circling it widely to move toward Ape City.

The Ape Council meeting was divided into three

sections. There were ten representatives of each species. The orangutans were older and more staid; Virgil was the youngest member. The gorillas were all brutish young males; Aldo was chief among them. The chimpanzees included both males and females; they all had kindly faces.

Caesar, Lisa, and Cornelius entered and took their seats on a dais before a table on which were stacked the apes' laws, a set of hand-lettered parchments. Caesar was deep in thought. He hugged Cornelius fondly and bade him keep quiet, then he called the meeting to order. He rapped the table for silence. "My friends, I have convened this extraordinary meeting of the council in order that I might report on an action that I deemed necessary: a reconaissance expedition to the Forbidden City..."

At that, all the apes reacted visibly. Lisa was startled and concerned. The gorillas became restless and fidgety, rattling their swords. The orangutans were outraged, and the chimpanzees were confused. The Forbidden City?

". . . with Virgil and MacDonald as my aides," Caesar finished.

"Why MacDonald?" complained Aldo. "Why not a soldier?"

"You will hear," said Caesar. Cornelius crawled under the table and stayed there. "When ape history comes to be written, we want it based not on legendary fiction but on facts. We went in search of records that might provide such facts."

"Did you find them?" asked a chimpanzee.

"Yes," said Caesar.

"And brought them back?" said an eager orang-utan hopefully.

"No," said Caesar.

"Why not?"

"Because we went in peace to what, we thought, was a dead city; but in case there might still be human survivors, we took MacDonald to parley with them and secure permission for our search." He paused. "There *are* survivors."

The Council murmured. "Survivors?" they echoed.

"Maimed, mutated, mad, hostile, and ... human."

The murmur became a shocked roar.

"They attacked us," said Caesar.

At that, the gorillas leaped to their feet. "Then let me lead my soldiers against them!" growled Aldo.

Caesar looked at him firmly, "General Aldo, not only are they armed, for they attacked us with sophisticated weapons ..."

"We, too, have weapons."

". . . but the radiation in the city is still such that if you and your soldiers fought there for just a few hours, you would become maimed, mutated, and as mad as they. So also would your future children."

The Council was shocked into silence. Then Aldo said sullenly, "Did the humans follow you *here?*"

"We saw no sign of it. But you are right to be concerned. We have to plan for a time when they *may* come out of the city, when they *may* find us."

Now the chimpanzees and orangutans rose to their feet; what was Caesar saying?

"Our gorilla army will exercise constant vigilance through continuous patrols. Civilians will assist in building defenses. And we should discuss training a militia."

Lisa gathered Cornelius up in her arms. "Caesar, is this necessary? Isn't it possible that the humans will stay in their city and leave us in peace?"

Caesar said gently, "Yes, it's possible. But if we wish for the peace to last, we must be prepared to fight for it."

Lisa turned desperately to Virgil, "Virgil. . . ?"

The pudgy little orangutan said calmly, "If light is possible, so is darkness. If peace if possible, so is war."

Caesar added, "This has not been an easy decision to make, but it is a necessary one. If we are to build a world of peace, we must survive. And if we are to survive, we must be strong." As this, the gorillas cheered.

Abruptly, there was a scuffle at the door, a flurry of sudden noise as a group of humans tried to enter. Two gorilla guards had grabbed them and were forcibly trying to evict them. The group included MacDonald, Teacher, Doctor, Jake, and a few others. MacDonald was resisting loudly, "Get your filthy gorilla hands off of me!"

"No humans in council," the gorilla was insisting.

"Stop that!" cried Caesar. "Release them!"

"Huh?" grunted Aldo and the other gorillas. They were standing, ready for a fight. Aldo turned angrily to Caesar; he stalked up to the front of the room to Caesar's chair. He towered over him. "No humans in council!" he roared.

Caesar remained seated. He spoke calmly, "They are here because I sent for them. Now that we know of the danger in the city, we need their help, their counsel."

"No," insisted Aldo. "No! No!"

The other gorillas also began roaring and pounding their tables. "No! No! *No!*" They began to chant: "No! No! No! No! No!"

Cornelius, intimidated by the gorillas, moved closer to his father. Caesar slipped his arms around the little chimp and stood up. He waited for the uproar to cease. After a moment the gorillas trailed off in their chanting. They weren't intelligent enough to be embarrassed, just uncomfortable.

Caesar said calmly, "*I* say yes."

The chimpanzees and orangutans, confused by the rapid pace of events, nodded their heads in agreement with Caesar; he seemed to know what he was doing. "Yes," they echoed. "Yes. Let the humans in council."

Cornelius relaxed, realizing that his father had won the point. Aldo realized it too; he was furious as he looked around the room and sensed the support for Caesar's position rather than his. He growled angrily as he realized that he had lost. He turned to the other gorillas, "Come! *We* shall not sit with humans. No!"

He strode from the room, and the other gorillas followed. At the door they shoved the humans roughly out of their way. They stamped loudly out of the room.

Caesar walked over to the humans. He clapped his arm around MacDonald's shoulder and led him, Teacher, Doctor, Jake, and the others over to the empty gorilla seats. He gestured them to sit down.

"Now," said Caesar, "let us reason together and make plans."

Méndez was saying to Kolp, "Governor, some-where along the line, this bloody chain reaction of violence has got to stop. A destroys B; B destroys C; C destroys A and is destroyed by D, who de-stroys E—and before anyone knows where they are, there'll be nobody left anywhere to know anything. Only nuclear dust, like those apes from the future predicted. The Earth will be a dead star."

Kolp's eyes blazed. "The star of our city is not dead. We shall live to see it rise again."

Méndez muttered, "At whose expense this time?"

As if in answer, Alma ushered in the travel-stained captain of Security, who had come directly to Kolp's office. He saluted sharply and said, "We found it, sir." He began to unfold a map. "The site of Ape City."

Méndez looked unhappy. Kolp seemed to grow. "Where?" he asked eagerly. "Where is it?"

The captain laid the map on a table. He began pointing. "There's a gorilla outpost here. Below that is a valley; it's planted with orchards and vineyards. There are orange groves and banana palms here. Enough to feed thousands." He tapped the map, "Their city is *here*."

"You saw it?"

"Yes, sir, we did."

"Did they see you?"

The captain shook his head. "No, sir. They were too busy. They seemed to be holding some kind of a council. Probably a council of war. I'll bet that Caesar was reporting to them on his reconnaissance. One day soon they'll be coming for us."

"No," snapped Kolp. "We're going for them. *Now*."

Méndez groaned.

"Go and alert your men. You know your orders."

"Yes, sir." The captain saluted and left.

Kolp beckoned to Alma.

"Yes, Mr. Kolp?" Her eyes were bright.

"Come with me. Méndez, you stay here and oversee the preparations." He led Alma out of the room. "I want to give you some special instructions."

"Yes, sir. Special instructions. *Oh!* Yes, sir!" She practically bounced along to keep up with him.

Kolp was in a state of fanatical euphoria. He half-strode, half-waddled, Alma beside him, through huge piles of supplies and scavenged materials from the ruined city. There were piles of rusty tin cans, pieces of ancient automobiles, old tires, bottles, stone columns, street and highway signs, street lights, and other useful and useless debris. The area was some kind of blasted tunnel, perhaps an old subway station. Now it was a warehouse, with mutants moving in frenzied preparation for the attack. They were pulling supplies from piles and loading dilapidated old trucks. There was a dusty school bus and a rickety-looking Cadillac. There were motorcycles and jeeps and even an armored troop carrier.

"We must destroy the whole zoo, Alma," Kolp was muttering. "Once and for all, we must destroy them. It is not enough to merely cage a dangerous animal."

"I don't quite ... I don't quite understand." She frowned.

He stopped and took her by the shoulders. She thrilled to his touch. "You will, you will." He pulled her through a side passage into a makeshift missile silo. The chamber was gray and featureless, strewn with rubble. And it was dominated by a huge cylindrical object.

Kolp gestured at it, expansively. "Beautiful," he sighed. "Isn't it beautiful?"

Alma nodded, without comprehension.

He turned back to her. "Alma, we've worked together for a long time, haven't we?"

"Eleven years and three months, Mr. Kolp."

"Yes." He stepped close to her, his eyes gleaming. "There's trust between us, isn't there?"

"Oh, yes," she breathed huskily. "Oh, yes."

"And more than trust—right?"

"Oh, yes." Her eyes were wide with anticipation.

"There's ... friendship ... isn't there, Alma?"

Alma sighed almost wistfully. "Yes, Mr. Kolp. There's friendship."

"Alma, will you undertake a task that I can only entrust to a true friend?"

"What task, Mr. Kolp?"

Kolp pointed at the huge object behind him. "Do you know what this is?"

"Of course, Mr. Kolp. It's our nuclear missile."

Kolp went up to it and stroked its shaft. "It's operational. Did you know that?" He gestured to her, and she approached timidly. He kept stroking the shaft of the missile as he reached out and took her hand. Her heart skipped a beat.

"Come closer, Alma," he whispered. She did so. "Touch it," he commanded. She extended her other hand and pressed her fingertips against the cold metal surface, then her whole palm. She began stroking the weapon in time with Kolp. The smooth steel felt so clean, so strong.

"If the impossible should happen, Alma," Kolp said. "If we're defeated by the apes, I will not surrender to animals." He squeezed her hand and held it tighter. "Neither will my soldiers. If retreat seems necessary, I shall send you a coded radio signal. Fifteen minutes after you receive it, you will range this missile on Ape City and activate it."

Alma breathed throatily, "Yes, Mr. Kolp, I will. I can do it from the main control console. What will the signal be?"

Kolp looked at her carefully. "Alpha and Omega," he said slowly.

Alma repeated, "Alpha and Omega."

He nodded. "You're a good girl, Alma."

She looked at him adoringly.

And at last he noticed her. "And a pretty one too."

They were still stroking the missile. Their hands moved together across its steel skin. Neither seemed to notice it any more, though. Kolp leaned forward, closer and closer, and kissed her. She kissed him back. Deeply. She stepped closer and slid her arms around his wide frame. "Alpha and Omega," she breathed. "I will be your tool."

Then and only then did Kolp take his slowly moving hand off of his weapon. He pulled Alma close against him and kissed her again. And again.

SIX

In Ape City the preparations blurred together.

Aldo inspected his troops. They were big and hulking and sloppy. They were dirty and hunched over, and they stood in long, irregular lines. The stench of them was unbelievable. But Aldo was happy. They were good, strong gorillas. But they needed weapons. "Guns!" insisted Aldo. "We need guns!"

Caesar directed the other chimpanzees and the orangutans in the laying out of borders and defense lines. They surveyed the areas around Ape City, trying to decide the best places for their troops to make a stand. They began building woven-branch walls across the slopes below the main part of the city. They brought in wooden furniture and heavy-looking carts as well—anything that could be used as a barricade.

Aldo trained his gorillas. They used swords and wooden shields; but they pretended that they had guns; they used sticks and branches and went through bayonet drill. They marched and practiced drills from the *Manual of Arms*. "We need guns!" insisted Aldo. He led his troops in mock battles against each other. Cavalry combat. Infantry attacking up ridges. Defenders holding off attackers. But always, "We need guns!"

Virgil organized a group of chimps and orangutans. They dug traps and covered them with branches and grass; they dug trenches and set stakes in them. Caesar oversaw the work and was pleased with it. He directed them to raise nets into the trees, so that they could be dropped down onto the road to entrap the enemy.

Aldo inspected his troops again. They were stronger than ever. And they were neater. Their lines were now straight and polished. The gorillas were a new *Wehrmacht*, fiercer and more horrifying than the one that had marched the Earth only a few generations before. Their black leather uniforms gleamed. Their boots gleamed. Their swords were raised in upright salute. And they shouted in unison: "We want guns!"

Lisa watched all of this and wept. She was angry and frustrated, torn between her love for Caesar and her revulsion for what was happening to the city and people she loved.

Every night when Caesar returned from his preparations, she pleaded with him. "On the night of the Fires," she said, "you swore an oath that in the future apes and humans would live together in friendship and peace. You swore that we would build a new kind of world, a world where there would be no war. Yet . . . yet, now you allow the gorillas to play at the war they've always demanded.

Don't you realize what a dangerous thing that is?"

Caesar didn't answer. He set his lip stubbornly. He sat in his chair and folded his arms.

Lisa tried to reason with him, "Caesar, haven't you seen how Aldo is training his troops? It's terrifying! And it means danger to us all! Don't you see? If you give the gorillas the means to make war, they're going to use those means. You've let Aldo train them into a terrible war machine. He won't be happy until he tests that machine and sees if it works. What if the people in the city *don't* attack us? What then? Aldo will still want to use his war machine—and he will! He'll use it against you. He'll use it against all of us!"

"No!" snapped the chimpanzee. "I am Caesar!"

"Do you think that will stop them once they make up their minds? You know how gorillas are!"

"I am Caesar!" he repeated. "And I say that I will control the gorillas. They will make war only with my permission!"

"But, Caesar—why? Why must we make war at all? Why must we make these horrible preparations? The people in the city might never attack us."

"They will!" he insisted. "I know they will."

"But *how* do you know?"

"Because," he began patiently, "unlike the humans in our city, those in the Forbidden City are mad. Mad enough to want not friendship and peace but enmity and war."

"Did they tell you that?"

"Yes," snapped Caesar. "By opening fire without giving us a chance to . . ."

". . . to explain why you were trespassing on their territory," finished Lisa.

"We didn't *know* the city was inhabited."

"Then how, if you never spoke to them, do you *know* that its inhabitants are mad?"

"Lisa, you haven't *seen* them. They're . . . malformed."

"Like the freaks in your foster-father's circus? Were *they* mad?"

Caesar opened his mouth to answer the question, but he was interrupted by Cornelius. The little chimp piped up, "What's 'malformed' mean?"

"Cornelius," said Lisa. "Go to bed." She went and turned down the blanket of his cot.

Cornelius dawdled. "I've got to give Ricky his water."

"Get into bed, young fellow," said his father firmly.

"Wait a minute," Cornelius said, concentrating on pouring water from a pitcher into a very small earthenware saucer. He inserted it through the cage door.

Caesar turned back to Lisa. "The freaks in Armando's circus were different. These people are the end-products of nuclear radiation. Their minds have been . . ."

Lisa gestured. A not-in-front-of-the-child gesture. She preceded Caesar to the privacy of their bedroom. Caesar followed her, insisting, "They're mutated, Lisa—and they're mad!" He slammed the door shut behind him.

The noise startled Cornelius' squirrel. Ricky jumped out of the still open cage and through the window. He scampered up a tree and into the night. "Ricky!" yelped Cornelius. He jumped for the window, then hesitated. He looked back. His first impulse was to call his parents, but their quarrel behind the closed door was still continuing. Noisily. Lisa was saying, "No madder than your gorillas. Aldo is bawling for guns."

Cornelius acted on his own initiative. He climbed out of the window. Still in his nightshirt, he scampered up the same tree after his squirrel. "Ricky," he called. "Ricky!"

The squirrel was chittering in a nearby tree. Cornelius grabbed a nearby vine and swung across, landing on a lower bough. Ricky looked down at him, chittered again, then turned and ran up the trunk. Cornelius scrambled after him.

Ricky stopped and chattered angrily. He ran out across a branch and leaped into the next tree. "Gorillas!" cursed Cornelius. It was the worst word he could think of. He followed the squirrel.

He landed in the new tree just before Ricky had leaped for a third. The small gray squirrel was a blur in the night, running and stopping, chattering and running again. He leaped from tree to tree, leading the little chimpanzee on a merry chase. Cornelius was always at least two trees behind. Up trunks, across boughs, through leafy corridors, along twining branches, and over into the next tree to do it all again. "Smelly gorillas!" said Cornelius.

Ricky went from tree top to tree top until suddenly he was in the last tree in the grove. There was no place left to leap to. He paused indecisively on the end of a long, thin bough. Beneath it glowed the embers of a campfire with hulking ape figures squatting around it. Cornelius began to stalk his pet, silently moving out along the bough. "Dirty, smelly gorillas!" he said to himself. The leaves of the tree kept getting in his way, but they concealed him from the figures below.

General Aldo, was busy haranguing his troops. "An army without guns has no power!" Aldo was insisting. There were animal sounds of assent. The gorillas nodded and grunted in agreement. "We need power!" Aldo growled.

Cornelius froze to immobility. Dirty, smelly gorillas, indeed!

"*Guns!* Guns are power. We shall get them," declared Aldo. "And we shall *keep* them!"

The gorillas agreed excitedly. They bounced and fidgeted restlessly. "Guns!" they echoed. "Yes, guns! Guns! We want guns!"

"With guns we shall smash humans—*all* humans!" Aldo's expression gleamed with eager anticipation. "And after that ..." He made a contemptuous gesture. "*... we smash Caesar!*"

Cornelius started at the sound of his father's name. The bough moved, so slightly that no one would have noticed it except Ricky, who, quick as only a frightened squirrel could be, leaped from the bough to the ground and escaped. He chattered into the darkness beyond the fire.

Automatically, the gorillas looked up.

And saw Cornelius. His nightshirt showed almost luminously white against the night. It reflected back the glare of the fire. So did his frightened face. He was clearly recognizable to the gorillas as he clutched his precarious position on the middle of the branch.

The gorillas froze. One or two jumped to their feet. Aldo was already standing, angrily glaring. "It's Caesar's son!" he declared.

The other gorillas rose silently, massively, to their feet, staring into the tree.

"He's been listening to us," said Aldo. Without thinking, he drew his sword. The blade flashed in the orange light.

General Aldo began to climb the tree.

Cornelius huddled against the branch and whimpered silently. His eyes were white with fear as Aldo came toward him, higher and higher, closer and closer. Aldo's face was rigid with anger. He held his sword between his teeth like a pirate. The gorillas watching from below grunted in support of their leader.

"Cornelius," said General Aldo. "Come down."

Cornelius shivered pathetically. He was too frightened even to shake his head.

Aldo growled and kept climbing. The tree swayed threateningly, and he paused. He surveyed the situation. The branch Cornelius clung to was too thin to support the weight of a full-grown gorilla. But maybe . . . maybe he could reach the chimp . . .

Aldo leaned as far as he could and made a grab. His big black paw missed Cornelius' foot by inches. He roared with frustration through his clenched teeth and made another grab. Again he missed. "Come down, you little . . . ! Come down, or else!"

He took the sword from his mouth so he could speak more easily. "Come down, Cornelius!" He waved the weapon threateningly. Cornelius only clung tighter to the branch. Aldo began flailing at him, trying to frighten him, trying to knock him down, trying to get the little . . .

Aldo stopped, suddenly realizing. Even if he did bring Cornelius down, the little chimp would eventually tell his father. And then Caesar and the other apes would learn of his ambitions. No, that wasn't a good idea.

Aldo's arm stopped in mid-stroke, nicking Cornelius' branch. Hmm, that gave him an idea. Suddenly, he knew how he could solve his problem.

He drew his sword back slowly and took careful aim. He struck. *Ka-thwunk!* The sword bit deeply and viciously into the branch. Again, *kathwunkkk!* The whole tree shook with the impact. The sword rang in his hand. Aldo took a firmer grip on the tree trunk for better leverage and began hacking steadily, firmly at the branch. With each stroke, Cornelius uttered a soft, childish whimper.

The big gorilla ignored the sound. He concentrated on his chopping. The blade bit into the bough, a little farther each time. His arm swung repeatedly up and down; his sword flashed over and over again.

"Father," moaned Cornelius. *"Father!"* His throat was almost paralyzed with fear.

Down below, the other gorillas watched. Their faces were marked with uncertainty.

Abruptly, the branch cracked—

"Father!" Cornelius screamed. "Father!"

Lisa woke suddenly and sat up straight. "What . . . ?"

"Huh?" mumbled Caesar, half-asleep.

"I thought I heard something. Cornelius?" she called.

Silence. She must have been dreaming. She settled down again.

And then the sound came again. A distant scream, cutting off abruptly.

This time Caesar heard it too. They both came wide awake now. "I dreamed he was calling for you," said Lisa. She got out of bed and ran for the next room, Caesar following close behind. "Cornelius!"

She gasped. His bed was empty. So was Ricky's cage. *"Cornelius!"*

Heedlessly, she ran from the room and swung herself down from the tree house. "That *was* Cornelius I heard!" Caesar followed her as she ran through the grove.

Ahead were two weaving torches moving in the same direction. MacDonald and Doctor.

"We heard a scream," shouted MacDonald to Caesar.

"It sounded like a scream of pain," added Doctor.

Caesar halted. "Cornelius is missing," he panted. Lisa didn't stop. She ran blindly, instinctively, toward the far end of the grove. Caesar, MacDonald, and Doctor moved after her; Caesar poured out a jumble of thoughts. "Ricky's cage was open. His squirrel must have . . ."

There was a terrible cry. A long-drawn wail of anguish.

"Lisa!" Caesar broke and ran. He forgot everything and dashed through the trees toward the sound until he came to the grove's end, where Lisa was sitting, cradling her son in her arms, like the legendary, long-lost Pietà.

She looked up at Caesar, tears streaming down her cheeks, and she could barely speak. "He's ... hurt, Caesar," she sobbed. "Horribly."

Caesar's knees gave way under him. He sank to the ground beside her. He felt weak and wobbly; there was an icy, sinking feeling in his stomach, and the world seemed to be shredding into little bits.

Slowly, he reached his hand out and gently touched his son, trying to discover how badly he was hurt.

There were a few apes and humans standing around, more arriving every moment. Doctor pushed through them, coming up to kneel beside Lisa and Cornelius. She looked tenderly at Lisa, "May I ... ?" she asked. Lisa nodded, almost imperceptibly.

At first Doctor didn't touch the little ape; he was so broken and pathetic. She had to determine what had caused his injury. She saw the broken tree branch, and that made her look up into the tree. The top of it was stark and broken; the jagged break a clawlike silhouette against the moonlit clouds.

Doctor bit her lip. She touched Cornelius now with gentle hands. Her voice was very soft amidst the murmur of apes and humans. "I think we'd better make a litter and carry him home."

As she rose and turned away, her face was marked with hopelessness. Caesar and Lisa didn't see it, and when Doctor turned back, her expression was more controlled. "I need some branches and a couple of shirts," she said and moved out to start picking some up.

MacDonald began picking up branches too. One branch in particular. He examined it closely.

His eyes narrowed. The break was too clean. Too sharp. There were hack marks in the wood.

Beneath him were the red embers of a campfire. The fire had been hurriedly and not completely extinguished. MacDonald kicked at them thoughtfully, suspiciously. He looked up again at the tree and frowned.

Behind him, the apes began to carry Cornelius home.

SEVEN

Lisa sat, almost in a trance, beside Cornelius' bed. Caesar sat nearby, his face in his hands. On the bed, Cornelius tossed and moaned.

Doctor stepped into the room. She sat down beside Cornelius, examined him, took his pulse, and tried to look like she was doing something helpful. As she rose to leave the room, Lisa followed her.

The chimpanzee touched the woman's arm. "Tell me the truth," she said calmly.

Lisa looked up at Doctor. Her face was so open and so trusting. Doctor said slowly, "He's all ... broken up inside." Her throat tightened as she went on. "Even if we had a hospital ..." She tried to finish the sentence, but couldn't. The words wouldn't come.

Lisa accepted it. Her large brown eyes remained clear, her manner firm. She touched Doctor's cheek gratefully. Doctor returned the touch. There was love and understanding between them.

Then the moment was over, and Lisa was turning sadly back to her son's room.

"Will you tell Caesar?"

Lisa stopped. "No. Not yet." She wore a strange little smile. "He still believes he can change the future." She went in to her husband and her child. She walked like a queen, determined and erect.

Far off, across the desert, the ruined city was coming to life. Ghouls that once were men were again walking the earth. Like the dead returning to life, like corpses climbing out of their graves, they were an army of living dead, echoes of a savage past.

Ghost trucks. Ghost uniforms. Ghost weapons. An ancient jeep and a mutant driver. A 105mm recoilless rifle, rusty and corroded, dangerous to fire, mounted on the back of the vehicle. Ammunition, cases of it, stacked around the mountings.

A troop carrier truck with torn and sagging canvas hanging on its sides. Shapeless men in shapeless uniforms. Red goggles, high black hats, scarred faces. Gleaming guns.

Motorcycles, several of them. Battered and dirty. Sputtering motors, loose, rattling chains, grinding gears.

A school bus. Incongruous. Listing to one side. Covered with dirt and dust.

A sagging black Cadillac from an unremembered year. Tail fins. Shattered rear window. Dented grill. Dirt.

Troops. Unable to bear light. Goggles, glasses, protective visors. Uniforms—not only military but postal, doorman, police. Weapons—rifles, pistols, shotguns, clubs, scythes, hoes, machetes.

Radio messages: "Keep all emergency channels pen."

"Yes, Mr. Kolp. All emergency channels open."

"Remember, Alma. Remember our signal."

"Yes, Mr. Kolp." A sigh. "I remember."

And motion. A sense of direction. Imperceptible t first, then a nudge, a gesture, a step, a movenent. An order: "Let's get moving!" A gathering f energy, a beginning of a feeling, a flowing, building wave, a surging crashing vector of savagery.

Explosion of action! Motorcycles were stamped o life. Engines coughed, then caught, then roared. The caverns smelled of carbon monoxide. The old netal came alive, sputtering, clattering, and banging. The walls echoed with mounting excitement nd noise—shouting, screaming, rumbling, battering, moving, climbing waves of energy roaring upward, out of the tunnels, out of the city!

And into the cold, cold desert. The night was black, the sky speckled with stars. Clouds of choking dust, clogging sand, slogging troops. The night was filled with the clatter of motors. The old engines choked and stuttered and missed, coughed and gasped and occasionally died, then coughed again and lumbered magically back to life.

An army of Lazaruses, they marched across the cold, glassy sand, a rag-tag gaggle of black-clad zombies. The vengeance of a dead city advancing toward the apes.

The sun peeked over the horizon behind them and began climbing up into the sky.

The desert began to warm up.

Within hours the glaring sun and the hot, reflecting sand had begun to take their toll. The desert heat was lethal.

The mutants sweated in their shabby uniforms, and the smell of their unwashed bodies was incredible. They moved in a cloud of stench that heralded their coming for miles, a stench of carbon monoxide, sweat, excrement, and decay.

Their vehicles limped across the desert. The engines rattled and popped, and occasionally one would pull out of the column and chug to a painful stop. When that happened—and it happened often —the mutants would abandon it, sorting themselves out into the remaining trucks and cars and jeeps.

Kolp raged and swore. He cursed and railed and lashed out at his men. Kolp was their fear, their anger, the fiery red hatred of a lumbering black beast.

The beast went rolling on.

The first apes to see the mutant army were two of Aldo's gorillas out on patrol. They were concealed behind a sand dune, staring across the desert, when they made the sighting. "Ah," grunted one, "look there." He passed a spyglass to the other.

"Humans!" growled the other. He snorted contemptuously at their trucks. "They'd move faster on foot."

The gorillas laughed.

The first gorilla pointed to the head of the advancing column. One of the black-clad figures, far in advance of the rest, had stopped to tinker with his stalled motorcycle.

The second gorilla made a noise in his throat. "Let's show them, huh?" He drew his sword and scrambled over the dune. Keeping low, ducking between the piled sweeps of sand, he ran toward the unsuspecting soldier.

His boots pounded across the desert floor. His eyes narrowed with purpose; his nostrils flared with determination. At the last moment he uttered a throaty scream of triumph. The man just had time to look up curiously.

The gorilla came charging down on him, hacking viciously at him with his sword as he had been taught by General Aldo. The man didn't even have time to scream—he just grunted. He crumpled slowly, a startled expression on his face.

The gorilla stood triumphantly over the dying body. He stamped his mighty feet and pounded his barrel chest. He roared and brandished his sword and shield and held them high. "Puny humans!" He screamed his defiance at the advancing column.

"Bring that gun around," Kolp was saying. He had his field glasses up to his eyes, studying the view ahead. The distant gorilla was now giving the body a few final hacks. "Dumb animal," muttered Kolp. "He has to demonstrate his bravery." Satisfied, the gorilla began loping back toward his position. The muzzle of the 105mm gun tracked with him. He had almost made it back to safety when Kolp said fiercely, "Fire!"

The weapon flashed.

The gorilla—no, there were two gorillas!—vanished in a high, towering explosion. The dunes shook with the mighty roar. Sand and rocks clattered through the dust and smoke to the desert floor. The dune had been replaced by a tremendous crater.

Kolp smiled in satisfaction. He lowered his glasses and grinned. Gorillas, huh? He gestured to his gunners, and they began to reposition the 105mm for traveling.

Had he kept his glasses to his eyes just a few seconds longer, he might have seen that one of the gorillas was still alive. Battered and wounded, but alive. The gorilla moaned and began dragging himself away.

In the apes' council room a deathwatch of humans, chimpanzees, orangutans, and one or two gorillas waited. MacDonald stood around with his hands in his pockets. Others stood or sat and muttered among themselves.

MacDonald looked up as Virgil came in. The little orangutan was shaking his head. "Doctor's doing her best," he said. "But I don't believe he can live. Caesar does, though. He refuses to leave Cornelius' side." Virgil looked at the man. "MacDonald, how can a benevolent god allow the branch of one of his own trees to crack and cripple an innocent child?"

MacDonald said bitterly, "It didn't crack."

The orangutan stared at him.

"It was cut," said MacDonald. "I picked it out

of the ashes of a campfire. The ashes were still warm."

"But who would want to hurt . . ."

There was a sudden sound at the door, and General Aldo came striding angrily into the meeting room. He was followed by two gorillas. One of them was injured and was being helped by the other.

Aldo stopped in the middle of the room and barked for order. The room quieted. The orangutans and chimpanzees moved to take their respective places at their tables. The humans followed, too.

Aldo waited until he had everyone's total attention. Then he said, "The humans have attacked and killed one of our scout gorillas."

The injured gorilla was helped to the center of the room. His uniform was ripped and spattered with dried blood. He moved with great pain. The chimps and orangutans reacted with consternation and confusion to Aldo's announcement and the condition of the gorilla scout. An old female chimp, elderly and dignified, covered her eyes and bowed her head. Behind her, a young male gorilla roared in anger and pounded the table before him. The room filled with gibbering and barking.

MacDonald realized the precarious position that he and all other humans were suddenly in. He rose to his feet slowly, very self-contained. "Where did this happen?"

Aldo looked at him and glared. But the injured gorilla said, "We were scouting the desert approaches to the city when we saw the army, still far away. They fired their guns. My companion was killed. I came to warn you." His voice was thick and uneven.

Virgil stood up then. "How long will it take them to get here?"

The scout shook his head. He didn't know, couldn't even guess.

Aldo spoke up. "Soon! They'll be here soon! So we must prepare *now!*"

He turned toward a group of uniformed gorillas, waiting at the door. He gestured at the human representatives on the council. "Take all humans out. Lock them up. Now!"

The gorillas moved quickly to grab the humans. Several of the men fought back, but the gorillas were stronger. Chairs were overturned in the scuffling, and blows were exchanged. The orangutans screamed at the outrage; the chimpanzees howled for order.

MacDonald, fighting the grasp of one of the bigger gorillas, shouted, "Aldo, you can't do this! You're acting against Caesar's orders."

Aldo considered this for a moment. Then he moved over to Caesar's desk, pulled out the chair and sat down. "Caesar is not here," he announced.

The gorillas hustled the humans from the room. They were brutal in their handling of men and women alike, shoving them roughly out the door.

The other apes sat by, helpless, unsure of what to do without Caesar there to lead them. Virgil rose and slipped out the back door.

The orangutan moved furtively through the settlement. Everywhere there were gorillas seizing control, roughly grabbing humans and rushing them off in the direction of the livestock compounds. A woman screamed as she was accosted by a uniformed gorilla. She dropped the basket of fruit she was carrying as he grabbed her and picked her up. Apples and oranges scattered in the street, rolling across the hard-packed dirt in all directions. The gorilla half-pulled and half-carried her along. Virgil stepped back into the shadows, so as not to be seen. Then he hurried on toward Caesar's house.

On the other side of the city, Aldo and another group of gorillas began pounding on a door. A wizened old orangutan opened a tiny grille and peeked out. "Who are you?" asked Mandemus.

"I am Aldo," declared the gorilla.

"What do you want?"

"We want guns!"

"And what will you do with them?"

"Whatever we want!" growled the gorilla. Behind him, his apes cheered. They began battering the door with a log.

"No!" shouted Mandemus through the grille. "This is wrong! Wrong! I am the conscience of the guns! You cannot . . ."

The door gave way. The gorillas came smashing through, barking and shouting, and pushed Mandemus aside. They filled the room with their massive bodies.

"Guns!" cried Aldo. "Guns! Now we have *guns!*"

The gorillas cheered and shouted and slapped each other heavily. They began to run through the room, ripping down racks and overturning crates of ammunition. They pulled open the boxes happily, splintering the wood with sharp, cracking sounds, and passed the guns and bullets from hand to hand to hand.

"No! No!" cried Mandemus. "No! You must listen to me! This is all wrong!" He moved from gorilla to gorilla, trying to make himself heard. They ignored him; they shoved him roughly aside and kicked him into a corner, then went on with their looting.

The gorillas came streaming out of the armory, their arms filled with weapons, yelling and looking as if they were celebrating some kind of holiday. It was a holiday. It was Gorilla Independence Day. "Guns!" they shouted, running wild through the city. "Guns! Guns! We have guns! We are the masters of Ape City!"

A band of gorillas came driving a small group of human workers down the street. The workers were bound together by ropes. One gorilla was leading, jerking the rope to keep the humans moving. Other gorillas kept striking at the humans from behind with their swagger sticks. The group was moving at a rapid trot.

After they passed, Virgil peeked out from behind a bush, looking both ways. Almost immediately, he ducked back. Ape City was now completely under the control of the gorillas. Galloping down the street toward the corrals was a gorilla on horseback, pulling a running man behind him on a rope. The human tripped and was pulled down the street by the gorilla. The gorilla looked back and laughed.

He kicked his horse in the ribs and urged it on to greater speed.

Virgil shook his head in sadness. All around him were the sounds of pathetic screams and cries—and the shouts of exuberant gorillas. The pudgy orangutan dashed quickly across the street to Caesar's house.

All the shutters were closed, and when he let himself in, he had to pause because of the darkness inside. As his eyes slowly adjusted, he became aware of Lisa, Caesar, and Doctor, clustered around Cornelius' bed. He moved to them and quietly touched Caesar's shoulder.

Caesar looked up, puzzled. It took him a moment to recognize Virgil, a moment longer to understand the urgency of his expression. He followed Virgil into the main room.

Virgil spoke quietly and intensely. "Caesar, forgive me . . . but you *have* to come."

"What do you mean?"

"Aldo has seized power."

Caesar shook him away. The whole idea seemed somehow trivial. "Let him. There is no power to seize. The council is the power." He started to turn back toward his son. "We can settle it later."

Virgil grabbed Caesar's arm. "Caesar! He's passing out guns! And he's ordered all humans to be imprisoned. The gorillas are rounding them up and driving them into the horse corral."

Caesar frowned. "What about MacDonald?"

"He was dragged from the council room by Aldo's gorillas."

Caesar shook his head slowly, unable to comprehend. "But Virgil, I can't leave my son. He needs me."

Virgil was insistent. "Every ape and human in Ape City needs you—*now!*"

"But . . ." Caesar raised his hands helplessly. The two apes stared at each other.

A thin voice broke the impasse. From the other room, Cornelius called weakly, "Father . . ."

Caesar hurried back to his son and leaned over him.

Cornelius spoke haltingly. "They . . . hurt . . . me."

Caesar wasn't listening to the words, though. He touched Cornelius' face gently. "Just relax, son." He smiled at the tiny spark of life that was his child, happy that it was still glowing, however faintly.

"They . . . want . . . to . . . hurt you."

Abruptly, the words registered. Cornelius was telling them that his injury was not accidental. Caesar stiffened angrily. "What? Who? Who hurt you? Humans?"

Cornelius' eyes closed, then opened again. He answered very weakly, "No."

"Then *who?*"

There was a long silence then, broken at last by a change in Cornelius' labored breathing. Doctor caught her breath. "Oh, no!" She knelt closer, but there was nothing she could do. Even Caesar recognized that now.

Cornelius suddenly opened his eyes again. His mind flickered back to a word he had heard. "Shall I be . . . malformed?" he asked.

Caesar said reassuringly, "No, my son. One day you'll be as tall as a king."

Cornelius smiled at the thought. The smile faded slowly on his face. His soft simian eyes closed again slowly. And didn't reopen.

Caesar touched the little body hesitantly. "Cornelius?"

But Cornelius wasn't there. There was nobody there at all. Just a small, broken body.

Caesar gave way to Doctor. The human woman listened for a heartbeat for a moment, then turned to Caesar and shook her head. Lisa wailed and threw herself across the bed, clutching hopelessly at Cornelius' tiny form.

Caesar's face twisted slowly from grief into rage. He stood up, saying, "They hurt my son. They killed him!"

Lisa continued sobbing on the bed. Caesar didn't even hear her. He rushed from the room angrily. He was totally distracted; he looked furiously from side to side. He rushed from the house in confusion. Virgil followed him, puffing to keep up.

Caesar started heading for the horse corrals. "He said . . . they hurt him. Who?" he muttered. "Who would hurt him?"

Virgil looked at the tall chimpanzee very seriously, almost afraid to speak. "Look around you, Caesar. You'll have your answer."

Caesar whirled on him, shook him fiercely. "Don't play word games with me, Virgil. What do you know?"

Virgil, shocked by Caesar's violence, shook his

head. He pointed at something behind Caesar's back. "That. That's what I know."

Caesar released the paunchy little orangutan, turned and looked. Looked at the gorilla version of a concentration camp. There was a large corral. There were prisoners. There were guards. The corral had been built for horses, but the prisoners were shocked and ashen-faced humans. Many were hurt. Some were lying on the ground, moaning. One or two were completely covered by blankets, still forms on the dirt.

The guards were gorillas, massive and black in their gleaming uniforms. Like elite troops, they strutted back and forth, automatic weapons cradled proudly in their arms. Others stood firmly at the gate, booted legs spread wide in a stance of immovability.

Behind them humans stood against the wire, looking out hopelessly. A small child peering out at a small chimp peering in. A cluster of men with long, matted hair, agricultural workers, squatting and smoking and looking at the gorillas with subdued hatred and resentment. MacDonald, Teacher, and Jake, standing close against the wire, scanning the passing apes.

"Caesar! Caesar!" MacDonald shouted suddenly, recognizing the distant chimp.

Caesar heard his name called. He started forward, toward the corral. He was horrified at this outrage. And there was Aldo, parading with his soldiers! Caesar's eyes narrowed, his lips curled back, baring his teeth. He strode angrily.

A loud, shattering explosion nearly knocked him

to the ground. He caught himself and whirled to see a pillar of fire and smoke rising from the ridge behind the grove. A towering black and brown cloud that cast its shadow across the whole city. Apes were frozen in their tracks, staring at it horrified.

Caesar closed his mouth and turned to Aldo and the rest of the gorillas.

"All right, you have your guns! Now let's see what you can do with them!"

Aldo turned from staring at the explosion and saw Caesar for the first time. "Guns, yes! We'll kill the humans! All the humans!" He barked at his troops to follow him. Quickly, he mounted his horse, wheeled it about and began riding down the main street toward the distant sound of firing. The noise came like a sporadic popping.

The rest of the gorillas shouted in triumph and waved their rifles. "We go to kill humans!" they cried, and galloped after their leader.

The battle had begun.

EIGHT

Another explosion shattered the afternoon, hurling rocks and chunks of dirt into the air. It was still far off, on the ridge of the gorilla outpost, but the city apes scattered in fright and confusion.

Caesar was already shouting orders, even while the thunder of the blast was still echoing through the valley. "Pile those wagons into a roadblock! Bring them down here!"

Chimpanzees and orangutans began scurrying to drag wagons and carts out to block the main road. Caesar and Virgil grabbed one of the nearest wagons, a massive heavy vehicle, and began dragging it toward the end of the street, toward the sounds of fighting.

The humans in the corral were forgotten. They pressed against the fence, watching the battle unfold before them.

Up on the ridge, at the gorilla outpost, a frenzied gorilla was trying to get his machine gun working. He fumbled with thick fingers, trying to unjam the frustrating gun, burning his fur and his skin as he did so. A second gorilla, still holding the belt he had been feeding into the gun, watched impatiently. Around them whizzed the bullets of the other gorillas. The rifles popped loudly.

Suddenly the mechanism was clear; the gun was unjammed. The gorilla shouted happily and jumped down behind the gun again, then fell to the ground abruptly beside the gun, his eyes glazed and startled.

Another gorilla seized the handles of the gun and, stepping over the body of his comrade, swung it around to face down the slope. He began firing in short, steady bursts.

Behind him other gorillas were firing their guns. Their automatic rifles rattled with staccato precision. But the gorillas were all badly shaken. They seemed ready to bolt.

The mutants came swarming up toward them. The column of vehicles rolled easily up the hard-packed road. Only the strongest of the mutant wagons had survived the trek across the desert, and now they came lumbering up the slope toward the gorilla outpost. Mutants were piling up toward the ridge, firing their guns and screaming, throwing grenades and occasionally falling and dying as gorilla bullets smashed into them. Here and there, a mutant would tumble backward, down the hill, but the main thrust of the mutant army was forward.

The mutants kept coming. The gorillas began falling back, edging up toward the top of the ridge. As the mutants drove them upward and backward, shells from the vehicles below began falling among them, cratering holes in the hillside.

For a moment, the battle hesitated as gorillas and mutants met face to face for the first time. The gorillas drew their swords and began hacking, only to fall helpless before the mutants' guns. And then the mutants rolled forward, onward, and upward.

The mutant army reached the crest of the ridge and teetered precariously. The gorillas were trying to make a stand.

From his jeep, far below, Kolp watched through his field glasses. His gunners kept firing the big 105mm rifle in a series of small, almost apologetic, coughs followed by massive explosions on the ridge, gouts of smoke and flame.

Suddenly the gorilla defense crumbled. The first gorilla broke and ran, followed by another and another. The mutants screamed triumphantly and chased them up the ridge and over. They poured over the crest of the hill, tossing grenades into the machine gun emplacements. The explosions hurled guns and gorillas into the air.

But then the gorilla cavalry arrived.

They came riding up from the valley below. Slowly at first, they rode four and five abreast. They came moving steadily down the road, building up speed as they headed toward the battle. They urged their horses faster and faster. They drew their swords and held them high. They screamed their challenges before them. Aldo was in the lead, shouting, "Attack! Attack! Kill all humans!"

As the cavalry roared up the road, they ran into

the gorillas retreating from the ridge. They scattered before the onrushing horses. The road ahead was almost jammed with fleeing gorillas, some walking, some almost running, some helping wounded comrades. But as they heard and saw the mounted gorillas approaching, they jumped for the sides of the highway. As the cavalry passed heavily through them, they stopped, began preparing places along the road to fight again. Some turned and began following the cavalry.

Some of the mounted gorillas were shocked at the sight of their troops in retreat; but Aldo and the other leaders only shouted louder, "Attack! Attack!" They waved their swords and urged their horses faster and faster. Hooves pounded harder on the road.

Watching them from the top of the ridge, Kolp smiled grimly. He lowered his glasses and remarked, "Here comes the circus. Monkeys on horseback. Get ready for the performance!"

The cavalry reached the bottom of the slope and began pounding up toward the ridge. Great clouds of dust rose up all around them. The charging black riders came galloping upward, a mounted, moving, thundering apocalypse.

The horses labored and puffed. The gorillas kicked them upward, heedless of their foaming sides and mouths. Flecks of lather spattered the riders. Dust clogged the noses and mouths of horses and gorillas alike.

And then they topped the ridge and saw a semicircle of automatic weapons trained on them. They were riding head on into the guns of the mutants;

the mutants were spread out across the top of the road.

Aldo was the first to react. "Off the road! Off the road!" he shouted. He signaled desperately for his troops to turn.

But it was too late, the cavalry had too much momentum. The riders in front were trying to wheel about; their horses were rearing in fright. The riders from the rear came piling into them; horses toppled and screamed. Hooves flailing, bridles jerking, they whinnied and turned.

And then the mutants opened fire.

The bullets slammed into the cavalry. Aldo and a few of the others managed to get out of the way of the hurtling hot lead. Aldo's horse leapt over a fallen log and crashed through the trees. Behind him, other gorillas and horses followed.

The gorilla cavalry lost its organization. More and more riders were arriving all the time, piling into the confusion and bloodshed; horses were moving in all directions. The smell of blood panicked them even more.

"Fire!" shouted Kolp. "Fire! Kill the monkeys!"

The gunners held their fingers down on their triggers, too shocked by the carnage ahead of them to stop. Horses stumbling and screaming, gorillas falling beneath them, more riders charging up from behind them, the ones in front trying to escape, trying to get out from under and back down the hill.

"Fire!" Kolp kept shouting. "Fire! Kill the monkeys! Kill them! Kill them!"

The cavalry was trapped between charging and

retreating, trapped between the automatic weapons of the mutants and their own, still arriving, rear. The cavalry died. Bloodily. Without honor. Without glory. In a savage, senseless, wasteful orgy of carnage.

They died violently. Without even the justification of having lived that way. They died for guns, and for Aldo's game. And there was no honor in their death. Only ugliness, hate.

The gunfire began to peter out. From a steady rattle of explosions, it degenerated into recognizable bursts, and then only occasional staccato blasts. Whenever anything moved—a horse trying to get up, a gorilla moaning, an arm or a leg jerking —it was silenced by gunfire. Soon nothing moved.

For a moment, there was silence. Only the smell of smoke and guns crackling as they cooled. There were occasional distant pops, and then even those were silent. The mutants' ears rang with the memory of the noise, and the heap of bodies steamed in the sun.

And now the road was clear.

Below, Ape City waited.

From the ridge, Kolp could see tiny figures running in and out of the trees. Chimpanzees, orangutans, and gorillas. Here and there, a horse ran riderless.

"We're wasting time," he said. "Let's finish it. There's a whole city of them waiting for us."

He leaned forward in his seat and signaled his driver to go on. The jeep lurched ahead, turned down the road. A couple of mutant infantrymen hung on the rear. A small advance force followed.

The bulk of the army would not be able to follow until they had cleared some of the carnage from their path.

Kolp's jeep passed around a clump of trees and the driver instinctively jerked to a halt. Kolp stood up in his seat and looked.

Below them were gorillas digging in and preparing to resist. Beyond stood Caesar's flimsy barricade of wagons. And beyond that, behind it, the main street of Ape City was visible for the first time.

"Yeah," grunted Kolp in satisfaction. "Yeah." He turned to his gunners. "There it is. When we leave, I want no tree standing, no two pieces of wood still nailed together—nothing left alive. Do you understand? I want it to look like ... like the city we came from."

He pointed down the road at Caesar's barricade. "First, clear that rubbish out of our path."

The gunner rammed a shell into the 105mm rifle. He swung it around in its mountings and took aim, squinting in the sunlight. He squeezed the trigger.

The valley echoed with the crash. A column of smoke rose where a wagon had been before. Now, there was only a crater.

The barricade was manned by chimpanzees, orangutans, and gorillas. They were crouching behind loaded fruit wagons and other farming equipment. Orangutans were dragging boxes of ammunition along, distributing it.

And Caesar sat behind a machine gun of his own. Virgil sat next to him, holding the ammunition belt, ready to feed it in smoothly when Caesar began firing.

"Here they come," said Virgil, looking up the road. A single jeep was just emerging from the orange grove. The jeep stopped and the gun on it began to rotate.

"Get ready to fire!" Caesar shouted to the other ape defenders. Forgetting himself, he rose to his feet, his teeth bared in a grimace of anger. He stepped up on the barricade, growling. Virgil pulled him back down just as another explosion shattered the barricade, an earth-rattling, ear-breaking, crashing thunder of a sound that splattered rocks and clods of dirt in all directions. Pieces of wood and flesh fell from the air.

Caesar grabbed his ears. He had never heard anything so loud! He picked himself up and began returning the fire. Still blinking from the force and sound of the explosion, he set himself behind his machine gun again and took careful aim at the jeep. He began letting off short bursts, testing the feel of the weapon, then longer ones. His lips curled back in rage.

But the jeep was too far away. Their bullets were falling short, and the 105mm gunner was finding their range!

Behind him, the other apes were moving to follow Caesar's example. They were stunned by the blast, but they moved to their places at the barricade and began firing, letting off single rounds with their rifles, unsure of what they were firing at, but firing anyway.

A third blast rocked the defense line. This was

the closest and loudest explosion of all. The noise
was incredible. The crash knocked the defenders
back, physically lifting them and throwing them
backward, shoving them to their knees. Smoke pil-
lared into the sky, dense and black and ugly. A
shower of things unidentifiable clattered to the
ground.

The ape defenders were stunned, shaken by the
force of the blast. Some dropped their guns in sur-
prise. Others gasped in horror and pointed.

Caesar lay sprawled on his back. Unconscious.
Covered with dirt and soot.

Some of the apes began to pick themselves up
and duck behind shelter, but most were confused
and terrified by the sight of their leader lying on
the ground. They stood milling about.

Virgil leapt to his feet and began running along
the barricade, shouting and urging the other apes
to pick up their guns. He grabbed a fallen rifle and
shoved it into the arms of a nearby chimp. The
chimp accepted it, but held it limply. He stood
there, staring back at Caesar's unconscious form.

"Get hold of yourself! Fight!" shouted Virgil.

"But Caesar—is he dead?"

"I don't know. It doesn't matter now. We've got
to defend the city!"

Another thunderous explosion shook the barricade then, hurtling wagons into the air. Jagged
pieces of wood, rock, and metal flew at them.

The chimpanzee dropped his weapon again and
abandoned the fight. He scrambled for Ape City
and disappeared into a tree house. Other apes be-

gan to break from their positions at the barricade, falling back away from the rain of deadly shells.

A loaded orange wagon exploded next. Oranges and fruity pulp splashed across the barricade, pummeling and splattering the deserting apes. All down the line now, they were turning from their positions, edging backward, trying to keep up a back fire. But to no avail.

An orangutan and a chimp ran for the cover of the city; they began clambering up into a tree house.

The tree exploded in a ball of orange flame, toppling slowly, tumbling, throwing the house clumsily downward, smashing it, and spilling its contents out onto the ground. The chimp and orangutan were nowhere to be seen.

From high on the ridge the bulk of the mutant army began to move, sweeping down the road toward the orange grove and Ape City. The trucks clanked and growled; the motorcycles sputtered; the jeeps banged and coughed as they swung down the last turn of the road toward the waiting victory.

Far ahead of them, Kolp's jeep and a smaller advance force were just crashing through the ape barricade.

Kolp was laughing with hysterical excitement. "Get them! Go on!" he shouted to his driver. "Keep going! Chase those stupid animals back to their trees!" He picked up a portable flame thrower. "Then we'll *burn* the trees!" The jeep plowed through the wooden barricade as if it were made of matchsticks. Kolp stood in his seat and torched the wagons and carts that made it up.

Delighted at the way they burned, he leaped from the jeep and danced happily down the line, flaming every wagon, every bush, every cart, every pile of wood, everything that wasn't already burning. Even the bodies of some of the chimp defenders. He aimed the torch at one, and it moved. Well, no matter. He started to pull the trigger anyway, then caught himself. He jerked the weapon aside so that even the short puff of flame that did escape would miss the ape.

He stepped forward curiously. "It *is* Caesar," he said.

Caesar opened his eyes then. He was confused, but he had heard his name. He looked around, struggling to focus.

Kolp towered above him, grinning. His radiation-scarred face had an almost unholy gleam; it was the reflection of the flames of the burning tree houses. Behind him, the rest of the mutants were setting their torches to Ape City. Kolp was still holding his flame thrower; it was pointed almost casually at Caesar. Caesar noticed that its tip was glowing hotly.

Kolp scratched his face thoughtfully. His grin faded as he surveyed the ape. When he spoke, his voice was harsh and grating, but his tone was conversational. Almost casual. "You and your people thought you destroyed my city, didn't you? But humanity survived. Look around you, Caesar. Men have returned to put apes in their proper places.

We are going to build a new world!" And with that, he loosed a short burst at Caesar.

Caesar twisted and rolled out of the way, but Kolp followed. "No apes at all!" he said, firing another burst. Again Caesar dodged. "No apes anywhere!" He jerked the weapon savagely and fired again. This time Caesar wasn't fast enough, the blast scorched his leg. Caesar backed away, trying to scramble, trying to rise to his feet. Kolp's driver knocked him back to the ground with a rifle butt.

And all around, there was silence. Kolp's 105mm gunners sat at their station in the jeep, tracking their gun slowly back and forth across the city to maintain order.

From above, and from the shelter of the trees—or what remained of it—the apes watched. Watched as their leader was humbled, humiliated, almost certain to be incinerated.

"No apes!" said Kolp, firing another burst. "No apes at all!" This time, he fired at Caesar's other side. He was guiding the ape, herding him, playing with him, turning him and moving him up toward Ape City. "You've forgotten what it is to have a master, haven't you?" Kolp punctuated his words with fire and flame. The smell of it was intense and stifling. Caesar's nostrils were scorched by the heat, and his eyes were watering from the smoke. His leg ached where it had been burned, and his head hurt where he had been struck. The rest of his body seemed weak and numb from the concussion that had knocked him out.

Above him, Kolp seemed to move in a cloud of gasoline fumes and flame. He belched smoke and fire, and his words blasted loudly through the red haze. "We could recondition you, Caesar. You could learn again what it is to have a master."

He guided Caesar up the main street of Ape City, his jeep and gunners following slowly behind. "No apes, Caesar!" Burst of flame. "No apes at all!" Belching fire. "No apes anywhere!" Blasting heat. "No apes except the ones we choose to let live!" Burning hate. "In our zoos! Would you like that, Caesar?" Belching burning hate. "Or as our *slaves!* Perhaps you would prefer that—to be a slave again. At least you would be alive ..." Red-fire-blasting, burning hate.

Heat and fire surrounded Caesar. He was confused and shaken; no matter where he tried to go, flames roared up in front of him. He was exhausted now. He was limping on all fours. He was crawling. He looked like an unevolved ape. "A slave, a slave," the thought echoed through his mind. "It would be so nice to take orders—no responsibility, no pain, no worry, no Aldo—no Ape City! No Lisa! No Cornelius—no Cornelius!"

Caesar stopped crawling. He stopped trying to get away. He stopped and looked back at Kolp.

Kolp noticed. And smiled. "Ahh, you're learning," he said. "That's good. You're a clever ape, Caesar. Very clever. Maybe, just maybe, you'll be one of the ones we let live. And then again, *maybe not!*" Another scorching blast of flame! Caesar twisted and dodged and tried to roll out of the way.

Kolp giggled at the sight. They were in the center of Ape City. Apes were all around him, on all sides, but not one had even dared move. None would. They were all staring aghast as he humiliated and destroyed their leader. After this, there would never again be an ape threat, not even an Ape City. They would be incapable of organizing. Ever. *If* any of them survived.

The ape crowd moaned with every burst of the flame thrower. They recoiled at every blast. They wailed and covered their eyes. One ape in particular—Lisa. Hearing the noise below, she had left her son's body and come to the window, only to watch in horrified silence, the slow, step-by-burning-step, hateful, painful torture of her husband.

Kolp was just loosing a blast. "Crawl, ape!" he shouted. "Crawl!"

Caesar didn't move. He stayed where he was, even though the flame was only inches from him.

"Crawl! I said, *crawl!*" Kolp's voice rose in annoyance and anger. This ape was spoiling the game.

Caesar only glared back.

"I am your master. You will obey me. You will crawl!" This bloody, stupid ape was going to defy him! But he was Kolp! No ape defied Kolp! No ape embarrassed Kolp, not in front of other apes!

Caesar just glared.

"Crawl, ape. I said, crawl, you hear? I'm giving you one last chance. If you don't start crawling, I'm going to kill you. I'll burn you!" Kolp's control was fraying. He was ready to end it now. He had to; the monster had defied him. "Crawl," he said one more time, gesturing with the flame thrower.

But Caesar was through crawling. He gathered

his strength for one last-ditch leap, a spring for Kolp. He tensed.

"All right! You forced me to do this. You did it yourself. It's your own fault." Kolp raised the flame thrower.

A voice, a shout! "No, Kolp, *no!*" A *female* voice. Alma? *Here?* He whirled.

It was Lisa, clutching the window frame. Lisa? Lisa! An ape? Saying "no" to him?

And then Caesar was on him, pulling him down, pulling at the straps that held the flame thrower in place. They struggled, rolling in the dirt, Kolp kicking and lashing frenziedly, Caesar clawing and grabbing.

Kolp kicked Caesar away, trying to free himself. He rolled, half-twisted, trying to place himself between Caesar and the other mutants, trying to hold onto his flame thrower. And as he rolled the machine went off. The tongues of flame lashed out and touched the jeep. The mutant driver and gunners jumped out, rolling to extinguish the flames. The gasoline and ammunition exploded behind them, enveloping the vehicle in a ball of orange fire and a cloud of greasy smoke.

The blast crashed through Ape City, hurling Caesar and Kolp apart. Kolp was thrown aside where he fell, dazed and unconscious. Caesar rolled and somehow, miraculously, found himself on his feet.

"Caesar!" A voice called. It was Virgil, shouting and running. He tossed Caesar a gun.

Caesar caught it, released its safety catch with familiar efficiency. Watching him from above, Lisa hid her eyes. Caesar let off a short burst at a small crowd of mutants nearby.

Then, suddenly, all the apes began to fire at the mutants.

Startled by the sudden defeat of their leader, the mutants were caught off guard. They began running back down the slope, down the road. They scrambled and tripped over each other in their haste to escape the angry apes.

"Come on!" Caesar was shouting to his comrades. "Let's fight like apes should! Come on! Kill the humans!"

All around him, chimpanzees and orangutans and gorillas cheered their support. They rallied around him and began charging after the fleeing mutants.

But more mutants were pouring down the road from the ridge. The bulk of the mutant army, a lumbering black mass of smoke-belching trucks, jeeps, and motorcycles, was heading eagerly toward Ape City. Kolp or no Kolp, they were bent on destruction.

The apes caught sight of this unstoppable juggernaut, and for a moment they faltered. They stopped in their tracks and moaned in fear. They wailed in fright, and one or two even dropped their weapons.

But Caesar was shouting, "Come on, apes! Defend your city!" And other apes, caught up in his passion, echoed his cries. "Get to the barricades! Kill the humans!"

The mass of the mutant army rolled on down the road toward them. They moved in a great cloud of dust and smoke and fumes, torching and burning whatever they encountered, leaving only ruins behind, heading inexorably for the apes.

They began letting off rounds, and the apes echoed their fire. The two armies were almost within range of each other now. They were about to touch—the barricaded apes and the rolling black *Wehrmacht*.

For a moment, the valley held its breath. And then Aldo and the surviving members of his gorilla cavalry, nearly a third of the original force, came down out of the hills above the road. They had regrouped and been tracking the mutants all the way. They appeared suddenly beneath the trees and came sweeping down on the unguarded flank of the mutant army, catching the mutants in a savage pincerlike movement between themselves and Caesar's angry apes.

Caesar's troops began firing at the suddenly disorganized mutants. Aldo uttered a throaty scream and charged. The gorillas waded into the mutants with flashing swords.

And machine guns! The gorillas had machine guns! And they knew how to use them. They fired indiscriminately into the mutant ranks at almost point-blank range. Horses fell, throwing their riders. They whinnied and fought for footing, stamping and kicking and trampling.

The mutant captains tried to organize their troops, tried to rally them. But even as they stood up and shouted, they were dying and their men were dying. It couldn't be done. The men scrambled to desert an ancient school bus as a round of fire blasted out its windows. The gorillas were

wielding their machine guns with a fanatic precision. A mutant on a motorcycle was chased by a
gorilla on horseback—it was Aldo!

The mutant crashed headlong into a truck as
Aldo's bullets chewed up the ground around him.
He fell to the ground and lay there without mov-
ing.

Then up from the barricades came Caesar and
the other apes. They came running to join the
fighting in the grove. Some of the mutants tried to
return the apes' fire from a stake-bed truck, but a
hail of bullets ripped through it, splintering the
wood and shredding the men.

Caesar led his apes onward into the thickest part
of the battle, always after the fleeing humans. The
mutants were starting to fall back, starting to retreat.

The mutant advance had slowed, then stopped;
the inexorable approach of the black juggernaut
had faltered, startled, stopped by Aldo's warfare.
Even now, the mutant *Wehrmacht* was trying to
back up, trying to put itself into reverse. But, like
a gigantic millipede whose nerve endings have suddenly become disconnected, the mutant army was
confused, disintegrating into its individual seg-
ments. Those in the rear were still trying to advance while those in the front were trying to retreat. They piled up on each other and even fought
among themselves.

The apes ran from tree to tree along their flanks,
always keeping cover, yet always keeping up a
steady hail of death. Other apes swung in the
branches above, firing down on the hapless men.

The mutants were running now, *openly running*, back up the road. Running and sometimes falling and dying. Some had lost their goggles and were trying to find safety in the shadow of the trees. They stumbled and groped and found only death as ape snipers picked them off. Others, despite their sun-startled blindness, lurched after their comrades. Gorillas, chimps, and orangutans all came charging after the retreating mutant army.

The mutants were in full retreat now. It was a rout. The vehicles coughed and sputtered and smoked and died. And the mutants abandoned them and kept running. They abandoned their guns and kept running. Anything to get away from those apes and their deadly, hacking bullets.

Some of the trucks and jeeps were still running. They rolled haphazardly through their own troops, men clinging to them, grasping for handholds, others jumping out of the way, the blinded ones not quite making it and falling under the wheels. Their screams were atrocious. The sound of their retreat was agony, with cheers of ape victory riding closely after them.

The apes came running and riding. They came with guns and swords and death. They came with vengeance. They came with Caesar.

The hideously disfigured men fled before them, riding when they could, running when they couldn't. The angry apes slaughtered them and left them where they fell, moving on to slaughter others.

And above it all, ahead of the other apes, rode Aldo. *General* Aldo! Proud and tall and waving his bloody sword! "Kill them!" he shouted. "Kill them all! Let no one get away!"

His gorillas echoed his cheer and charged after him, charged eagerly ahead, screaming and trampling the fleeing men, firing and killing. Cheering and laughing.

Caesar and the other apes stopped at the ridge, at the ruins of the old gorilla outpost. But Aldo and his horseback troops rode on, still raiding the mutant army from the rear. They would ride in and separate a small pack of men, surround them, circle them like Indians around a settler's wagon, the circle always getting smaller and tighter, like a noose, the mutant army always getting smaller. The gorillas would circle and kill, firing their blazing hot guns, slashing with their heavy iron swords. Circling and killing until the last man was dead. Then, cheering at their victory, laughing with the joy of it, the gorillas would reload their guns, heft their swords anew, and go charging again into another pack of frightened, running men to repeat the performance.

Again and again they did this. They chased the mutants across the desert until there was no longer a pack, just a disorganized rabble, scattered men all running in the same direction.

The gorillas rode them down. They charged across the sand, their horses' hooves pounding like thunder. They came like a very devil and ripped into the terror-stricken men where they found them. They trampled the men, beheaded them, shot them, sliced them, and hacked at them.

The men scattered like cockroaches, and the gorillas went galloping after, a pack of them howling after every one, hunting them down as men once hunted animals.

In the desert, the radiation-torn survivors of the last human war at last met their final destiny. Each man died alone. The gorillas laughed at the humans' lonely, painful deaths. Then wheeled their horses about and went looking for more to kill.

They would be at it for hours, all the way across the desert. And of the vast human army not one man would survive.

NINE

There were three who survived the battle. But they would not survive the war.

Two were no longer soldiers, would never be soldiers again. They were just two frightened men, managing somehow to elude the marauding gorillas, managing somehow to make it back to their blasted city.

They were wounded, and they had lost a lot of blood. For the last few miles they had to hold each other up, and they made it on will power alone. But they got far enough to deliver their message. They made it to the tunnels, where they finally collapsed and died.

But that was message enough.

The message was that they had lost the war.

When Alma heard about it, she went to look at the bodies. She surveyed them without emotion. "I know what I have to do," she said.

Beside her, Méndez was appalled. "He said to wait for his signal."

She pointed at the bodies. "I've just received it." She turned and strode purposefully down the hall.

The third man was Kolp.

Ragged and exhausted, he went stumbling head-long across the desert. Back to his own power—Ape City *would* be destroyed! He still had one weapon left.

He lurched across the sand, muttering orders to nonexistent troops. How he had escaped from the apes he didn't know. He couldn't remember. He only remembered walking, running, fleeing. No, not fleeing! Kolp wouldn't flee. Kolp must have walked out like a man.

That's it. Kolp had walked out like a man. Dazed, battered, confused, shocked, bloody.

The apes had been too busy to notice him, pre-occupied with their side of the slaughter. He had gotten up and walked out, startling those who had seen him but encountering no interference.

Somehow he had made it through the orange groves. Somehow he had made it over the ridge. And somehow he would make it across the desert. To his city. To where the Alpha-Omega bomb waited.

He staggered on, blind and deaf to the carnage around him, to the burning vehicles, abandoned where they had stopped, to the strewn bodies of his troops, their blood drying on the sand. He moved through them, not seeing them, refusing to see them. The sand was littered with death.

It wasn't until he stumbled over a broken rifle

that he began to realize. He held the weapon curiously, looking at it for a long time before he recognized it as a gun. He didn't notice that it was broken, that it would never fire again.

"My army," he said. "One of my troops has lost his gun." He looked around him, still not seeing the scattered bodies. "One of my troops has lost his gun!" He shouted it loudly. "Where's my army? Come on, there's a war to fight! Pick up your guns! Let's go!"

He began exhorting them. He waved the rifle weakly over his head, a shadow of his former fury. "Kill the apes! Get up, you sluggards! Kill the apes!" He stumbled, caught his footing, and went on. "My army is the best in the world! Let's kill the animals! Kill the dumb animals!"

There was something ahead of him. He staggered toward it, still babbling: "Kill them! Time to regroup! Counterattack—get them with the big guns. The biggest guns. Kill them!"

He lurched into the object and stopped. It was a horse. "Horse," he said, steadying himself against it.

And rider. Kolp looked up. Aldo stared back, frowning, puzzled.

Kolp blinked confusedly. "Gorilla?" And then he realized. He fumbled with the broken rifle; he was still carrying it, had forgotten to drop it. He tried to raise the weapon and take aim.

Aldo's bullets caught him where he stood, spun him about, punched through him and hurled him ten feet across the sand.

Kolp was one of the lucky ones. He died without pain. As he had lived—without feeling.

Aldo grunted in satisfaction.

"Now we go home," he said. "To *our* city. *Gorilla City!*"

Alma's hand rested on the missile control console.

Méndez' hand came down on top of it.

"Alma! For pity's sake! Wait for the governor's signal."

"He's dead," she said tonelessly. "They all are. We would have heard by now. This is how he would have wanted it." Her hand strayed across the surface of the panel.

Méndez grabbed it again. "Alma! Hasn't there been enough killing?"

"No!" she shouted back at him. "No—there hasn't! They killed Kolp! Those apes killed my Kolp!" She jerked her hand away from his grasp. Her voice rose in pitch. "They destroyed our city and left us with nothing but ruins, and now they've taken Kolp from me and left my life in ruins! There's nothing left for me! I want them to die!"

Méndez took a step toward her, but she backed away, toward the bomb.

"Alma, listen to me!"

"I don't want to! You'll only try to confuse me! You'll tell me things I don't want to hear about! I don't want to hear your facts! Kolp told me what to do, and I'm going to do it." She stopped against the cool metal of the tall, silvery bomb.

Méndez spoke quietly, calmly. "Alma, come

away from there. Let's leave here, now. Just listen to one thing, listen to me. If you really do want to destroy the apes, you can destroy them anytime. This missile will wait. So can you. Just wait a few days, a week even. Give Kolp a chance to come back. Give yourself a chance to think about it. Make sure it is the right thing to do."

"I have thought about it!" Her eyes blazed. "It *is* the right thing to do! Kolp told me!"

Méndez took another step toward her.

She took a step backward, moving around the missile. Suddenly she froze. "Oh, no . . ." she whispered.

"What is it?" Méndez came around the bomb to look. She let him; she made no effort to move away. Instead, she pointed at the dull black letters painted on its side: "ALPHA-OMEGA NUCLEAR DEVICE."

"So that's what the signal meant," she gasped. "He never told me."

"The final weapon," said Méndez. "This is it, the final weapon. The *last* bomb!"

"He never told me." Alma echoed.

"If he couldn't win, he was going to let the whole world lose," said Méndez. "He was . . . he was mad!"

"Oh, no," moaned Alma. "Not, not . . . not . . . *mad*. Please, not *mad!*" She covered her eyes, sobbing.

Gently, Méndez pried her hands away. "Face it, Alma."

"No, no, no, not mad. *Not* mad." She looked up at him, eyes wet. "I'm not mad. *Please*. I'm not mad. I just didn't know. I didn't know, that's all. Please don't let them hurt me."

"*Alma*, you know what this is, don't you?"

She nodded. Slowly.

"Tell me."

She shook her head. "No."

"*Say it!*"

"Nooo!" she moaned.

He slapped her. Hard.

"It's the Alpha-Omega bomb. It can destroy not only the apes' city but the entire Earth." Suddenly, she was babbling. Almost hysterically. "Activate it and we become nothing. Leave it and its very presence will insure that at least we remain *something*—and may become something better." She repeated everything she had ever heard about the device. "Mankind must never, never detonate the bomb. Never!"

"Alma," Méndez stopped her. He held her by the shoulders and looked directly into her eyes. "You are *not* mad. Do you understand me? You are *not* mad."

"Not mad," she repeated.

Méndez realized then that they were not alone. A small crowd of curious men and women had entered the silo.

He turned to them. "Listen to me. We have been reborn today. This missile, this device, is a symbol of our rebirth. We must venerate it as a responsibility, a responsibility that our ancestors entrusted us with. We were given that responsibility because we are *human*. Because we are human, we are beautiful, we are good."

"We are beautiful," the crowd echoed. "We are good."

His face was scarred, his skin ravaged by radiation, but his eyes glowed with a holy mission. Méndez raised his hands and proclaimed, "We are men! We are human!"

And again the crowd echoed him.

Only Alma was silent. Her gaze kept straying back to the bomb. But whatever she was thinking about remained unspoken.

TEN

Ape City was a shambles. Trees were scorched and toppled, some still burning. The sky was clouded by black smoke from the fires. And there were too many bodies. The chimpanzees were beginning to clear them up. But there were too many bodies. Caesar's chest ached at the sight of it.

He strode slowly up the long street, Virgil beside him. He was heading for the horse corrals. As he came into sight, the humans there began to rouse. They recognized him and began to cheer and call his name.

At the sound, other apes, chimpanzees and orangutans especially, began to come out of their tree houses or look up from their work. They began to cheer Caesar, too.

Caesar didn't acknowledge their accolade. He didn't wave, didn't smile, just kept walking toward the corral. His face was grim. His body ached, and his arms and legs were sore. He was tired and numb and still shocked at the carnage he had participated in, even encouraged. He had thought—no, prayed—

that he had fought his last battle nine years before.

Behind him, the cheering grew louder. He ignored it until he heard the sound of galloping hooves thundering up at his back. The gorilla cavalry was returning.

Caesar didn't bother to look around. He hurt all over. He didn't want to hurt any more. He walked the last few steps to the corral and stopped. The humans inside looked at him expectantly. He started to move, then realized he just didn't have the strength. "Virgil," he said. "Open the corral. Let them go. Let them all go." And then he turned to look at the approaching gorillas.

Virgil started to undo the bolt, but General Aldo came pounding up on his horse, shouting. He jerked the animal viciously to a halt, spraying Caesar and Virgil with dirt and rocks; the animal reared once and whinnied in protest, but the gorilla ignored it. He dismounted angrily. "No!" he growled at Caesar and Virgil. He pointed at the humans. "They stay in corral!"

The two apes looked at him.

Aldo thumped his chest. "Aldo will say what to do now!"

Caesar shook his head. "These people did nothing. They can go free."

Aldo sneered. He looked Caesar over as if he were no longer worth arguing with. "I am General Aldo," he said calmly. "I give orders." His expression changed slowly. "You like humans? You want them not in corral? Okay, good—I fix." He turned to his gorillas, his elite troops who had ridden with him across the desert. They were covered with dust and blood, laughing in their murderous glory. "Kill them!" barked General Aldo. "Kill them all! Kill the humans!"

The gorillas raised their guns to fire into the corral. The humans, terrified, backed away, cringing, some of them moaning with fear.

Caesar stiffened in outrage. Then he seemed to grow in stature. The gorillas stared at him, waiting to see what he would do. Despite his wounds, his numbness, and his shock, he managed to stand tall. He hobbled over to stand in front of the gate, between the humans and the gorillas' guns. Something about his manner made the two gorillas guarding the gate edge away; they moved to stand with their fellows.

Caesar spoke slowly, and when he did, his voice betrayed his exhaustion. But his words were firm. "There will be no more killing, Aldo. Put down your guns. Take them back to the armory. The war is over."

Aldo's anger rose. How dare Caesar speak to General Aldo this way? But he controlled himself. Even his most loyal gorillas were startled by this sudden face-to-face confrontation and might hesitate to shoot Caesar. But Caesar was only a puny little chimp, hardly bigger than Cornelius. Aldo was stronger. Aldo would win. He was general of all the gorillas, and he was in charge now. His chest swelled as he declared, "No! We keep guns now. Move! Or we kill you!"

Caesar shook his head. Beside him stood Virgil. And now Lisa. And Doctor. The four faced the gorillas. A crowd of chimps and orangutans watched, shocked and horrified.

Virgil spoke for Caesar. "Ape shall never kill ape ..." It didn't really need to be said, but the next part did: "... let alone an ape child!"

Aldo's eyes narrowed. He sneered. He raised his hand as if to give the order to fire, but behind him the faces of his gorillas showed that the meaning was beginning to sink in. Ape shall never kill ape! Holy words! Yet here they were with their guns pointed at Caesar and Virgil and Lisa!

And Cornelius! Their faces betrayed their realization! Aldo had killed Cornelius!

The rifles wavered.

The gorillas frowned in confusion, puzzling over this terrifying new thought. Apes were better than humans because apes didn't kill. Apes never killed apes! But Aldo ...

They looked at their leader, aghast.

One of them stepped out of the line. He pointed and gestured inarticulately. "Aldo ... Aldo ..." But he couldn't, just couldn't bring himself to utter the deadly words, the ultimate accusation. The thought kept catching in his throat. Behind him, other gorillas began muttering, began pointing and whispering and grunting nervously. "Aldo ... Aldo ... Aldo ..."

Aldo whirled to stare at his troops. "Get back in line!" he shouted. "Back in line!" But his self-confidence was faltering. They ignored him, and he became flustered. He looked from side to side, as if seeking aid—or an exit.

"Aldo has killed an ape child," Virgil declared

loudly. "The branch did not crack. It was cut by Aldo's sword!"

Around them the apes gasped. Chimpanzees wept. Orangutans barked in angry reaction. All recoiled as if struck.

Aldo snarled at the accusation and the accuser. His expression froze into a hateful glare. His lips curled back in fury. His posture became more savage, more brutal. Deep in his throat he began making a deadly sound. Aldo had become an animal, a total animal. All pretensions of intelligence had fled in his murderous urge to survive and conquer and kill.

All around him, the apes were pointing. Pointing and staring and muttering among themselves. There was no escape.

In the corral the humans were silent and wide eyed. Except for MacDonald, who murmured softly, "Welcome to the human race . . ."

The words touched Caesar's ears, and he straightened. Yes. Welcome to the human race. Welcome to killing and hatred and war. Welcome.

Around him the muttering and whispering was dying out. All were waiting for him to act. He shook off Lisa's attempt to hold him back and took a step toward Aldo. "You . . . murdered . . . my . . . son!"

Aldo's eyes were wary. He was an animal at bay. He began to edge backward, away from Caesar. Caesar kept moving forward. He was unarmed but he didn't need a weapon, not now. Weapons were for the weak in spirit.

Aldo drew his sword, the same short sword he

had used to chop away Cornelius' branch. He swung the sword around and pointed it at Caesar.

Caesar didn't pause. He kept moving toward Aldo.

Aldo kept backing away until he could back no more. He held the sword out in front of him.

Watching, Lisa moaned in fear. Behind her, two of the humans, Jake and MacDonald, were wrenching loose a length of chain that had been entwined in the corral fence. MacDonald wrapped it in a ball. "Caesar!" He threw the chain.

Caesar saw it coming. He sidestepped it as it hurtled past, then scooped it up from the ground. He turned back to Aldo. He started swinging the chain to knock Aldo's sword from his hand.

But at the sight of the heavy metal links, Aldo panicked. He remembered too well the chains that the humans had put on him so many years before. Now they wanted to chain him again! He broke and ran, pushing his way through his gorillas. He ran for the trees.

Caesar broke into a run, too. The apes cleared a path for him to pass, then flowed after him.

Aldo picked a tree and was up it. Seconds later, Caesar followed. Aldo was up there, terrified now, crashing his way through the heavy branches. Caesar paused and listened. Yes, there he was. He scrambled after.

Aldo stopped near the top; the branches bent under his weight. He cast around nervously for an escape. Caesar was coming! The branches creaked precariously, announcing his position.

Caesar's face appeared suddenly below him, then

his hand—the chain was wrapped around it. No! Not the chain! He shifted his position so that he could swing his sword.

Caesar peered upward. The sunlight was glaring, turning the treetop into a weird jumble of shapes and flashes. He squinted, trying to make out Aldo's form in the glare. Trying to . . .

Wfffftt—thunk! Aldo's sword bit into a branch only inches from Caesar's hand.

Without thinking, Caesar swung upward with his length of chain. Aldo leaped to avoid it, but it struck him on the leg. He jumped, but the branch supporting him cracked and gave way.

The crowd below screamed.

But Aldo had managed to grasp a limb of another tree. For a moment he hung there precariously swinging back and forth. Then he swung himself up and moved rapidly across the treetop, leaping across to a third tree.

Caesar followed. Inexorably.

The two apes moved from tree to tree, Aldo fleeing, Caesar pursuing. They moved without words, just an occasional grunt as the air was forced from their lungs by the impact of grabbing or landing on a branch.

They were getting to the end of the grove now. Aldo stopped and turned, jabbing with his sword as Caesar came climbing. He struck and caught Caesar on his side! Then Aldo leaped free as Caesar swung his chain.

Caesar ignored the pain. All he could think of was Aldo—and Cornelius! He kept following. Aldo had moved into the last tree of the grove.

This tree was comparatively isolated. Caesar made his way along the branch of the nearest adjoining tree, trying to figure how he could best make his attack. The branch he was on was a thin one, it began to crack and break, making Caesar's decision for him. As it fell away, he made a great leap and an arm-wrenching grab.

He was clutching a branch of Aldo's tree, heaving himself into it, moving in after Aldo. There was no other tree for either of them to move to. Caesar began closing in on Aldo. Aldo clutched his sword and waited.

Caesar paused, listening for the gorilla's heavy breathing, then moved in. Aldo began swinging his sword, slicing the air, reaching and slashing, trying to kill, to maim, or even to halt the inexorable advance of the murderous Caesar. He was backing along a thick, wide branch, always keeping Caesar at arm's length—but only with great effort. His sword was *getting too heavy*. He wished he could drop it, wished he could be free of it. But *no*, he was a gorilla! The sword made him strong! He kept jabbing and poking and slashing.

Caesar countered with his chain, swinging it through the air, trying to knock the sword from Aldo's hand, trying to knock Aldo from the branch. He swung again and again.

Aldo backed away. He had reached the end of his branch now—he could go no farther. He raised his sword as if to throw it.

Caesar paused and surveyed the situation, cocking his head and frowning.

The branch creaked and bent. Aldo tensed.

Caesar moved. He brought his chain around.

Aldo *struck*. He slashed viciously forward, slicing a wicked gash across Caesar's chest. Caesar toppled backward, grabbing another limb close to the main trunk. But even as he fell, he swung his chain. It wrapped itself around Aldo's head.

Aldo fell.

The fall seemed to take forever, the body crashing downward through the branches, each impact brutal and graphic, the last one, the most awful of all. Aldo hit the ground with a thump. He lay motionless, his eyes still furious and staring.

Caesar began to climb down. He dropped slowly from branch to branch, the blood leaking from his chest and side. He fell the last twenty feet, landing on top of Aldo's broad body.

Almost immediately Lisa and Virgil were at Caesar's side, trying to help him up. He shook them off. He rose to his hands and knees by himself and found himself staring into the sightless eyes of his enemy. At the sight of Aldo's face a wave of nausea and exhaustion swept over him. He allowed himself to accept Virgil's help and stood unsteadily, supporting himself on the shoulder of the paunchy little orangutan.

"Virgil," he murmured. "You are the philosopher. Tell me—should one murder be avenged by another?" He looked down at Aldo. "I am no better than he. I have killed too."

And then he collapsed.

He slipped to the ground in exhaustion, Virgil trying to hold him up, but failing. Doctor and Lisa came rushing in to attend him. "Get some water," Doctor said. "And some bandages and a splint."

"He'll be all right?" Fear edged Lisa's voice. She had lost too much already.

"Yes, I think so," said Doctor.

But Virgil murmured, "No, none of us will ever be all right. Never again."

ELEVEN

But Virgil was wrong.

When Caesar went to break the lock on the horse corral and free the humans, an odd thing happened.

They didn't leave.

They didn't pour out in an eager stream; they didn't thank him or acclaim him. They just stared and waited.

Caesar frowned, puzzled. He didn't understand.

"You can come out now," he said. "You are free."

MacDonald stepped slowly forward at that. "Free?" he asked. "Free to do what apes tell us to?"

Caesar blinked, confused.

"If you really mean to set us free," said MacDonald. "Then free us completely."

"But ... but ... we have always treated you fairly. Much better than you ever treated us."

"That was the past, Caesar. That was another time and another people. Two wrongs don't make a right. One slavery does not avenge another any more than one murder avenges another." Caesar flinched at that.

Caesar turned to Virgil and Lisa and the other apes behind him. Looking for support. But their faces were as confused as his. He turned back to MacDonald and said slowly, "The human way has always been one of violence and death. Humans came across the desert to kill us."

"And who slaughtered them from horseback?" retorted MacDonald. "Who chased them across the desert till there were no survivors?"

"That was Aldo and his gorillas!" snapped Caesar.

"And who slaughtered Aldo?" asked Virgil from behind. His tone was quiet but firm.

Caesar whirled, momentarily startled, then seeing the little orangutan, his face softened. "Virgil, you are a wise and good ape. But . . ." He raised his hands helplessly. "What can I do?"

MacDonald answered his question for him. "Trust us."

Caesar looked at him. "Trust you?"

"We want to have honor, too. We want to live with respect. We will live as your equals, Caesar, or life will not be worth living at all."

"There is everything to gain . . ." murmured Virgil.

". . . and nothing left to lose," finished MacDonald. "Remember . . . the last war?"

Caesar's body ached from his wounds; but his head hurt even more with the weight of the decision he had to make. "Trust you?" he asked MacDonald. "Trust you?"

"You have no choice," insisted Virgil. "We need their help, their hands, and their hearts to rebuild Ape City. We have to trust them. All apes have to."

"No," said Caesar. "Not Ape City, not any more. Now it has to be *Our* City. All of ours. If we accept their help, then we must accept them as well. All of them. It will not be easy, but let us start here." He turned to MacDonald. And held out his hand.

MacDonald grinned. He stepped forward and took it.

And then the humans did stream out of the corral, cheering and shouting. And crying too. But the tears were tears of joy.

As the last gun was cleaned and oiled and put away, Mandemus came to Caesar.

"Caesar, I must ask a favor. This armory has been my home for many, many years."

Caesar misunderstood. He put his hand on Mandemus' shoulder. "You may live in it until the end of your days, old fellow. You have earned it."

"No, no!" insisted the wizened orangutan. "I don't want to live in it! I want to be free! Now that the danger is over, I want to see this accursed storehouse and everything in it destroyed! Blown up!"

"So do I," said Caesar. "But we mustn't. We can't. The greatest danger of all is that the danger is never over. Mandemus, you must stay here and continue to be our conscience. If we are to be free, we must be responsible. Help us be responsible."

Mandemus sighed, "You will never understand, Caesar, will you? As long as there are weapons here, there will always be danger."

Caesar looked back at him. "No, *you* don't understand. As long as there are weapons *anywhere*, there will be danger. This armory must stay here, always ready, always waiting."

"Waiting," muttered Mandemus. "If a weapon is made, it will be used. Caesar," he said, "I do not think we have won the war. The weapons have." And with that, he turned and disappeared back among the cases and crates of death.

Waiting. Like a distant bomb, with "Alpha-Omega" painted on its sides. Waiting. Like the woman, no longer mad, sitting, staring. Her hand on a console. On a button. Waiting.

EPILOGUE

Many years later, many centuries after the fact, a lawgiver stood on a hillside and taught a class.

"We still wait, my children. The weapons still wait. The danger still exists. But each new generation is a renewal, a renewal of the promise that we can survive together. We must. Or none of us will survive at all."

He closed his book softly. "The promise is yours to keep. Yours to pass on to your children for them to keep." He looked over his class and smiled. "We have not done badly so far."

The rapt faces of ape and human children stared back at him. Chimpanzees, orangutans, and gorillas, blacks, Orientals, and Caucasians. All together . . .

AWARD

MIND-SHATTERING SCIENCE FICTION

MEN AND MACHINES　　　　**Edited by Robert Silverberg**
Unforgettable science fiction masterworks by Lester Del Rey,
Robert Silverberg, Fritz Leiber, James Blish, Brian Aldiss and
other greats.　　　　　　　　　　　　　　　　　**AN0765—95¢**

THE ENDS OF TIME　　　　**Edited by Robert Silverberg**
Compelling, brilliant science fiction from Poul Anderson, Robert
Silverberg, Fritz Leiber, Arthur C. Clarke and other masters.
　　　　　　　　　　　　　　　　　　　　　　　AN0778—95¢

TOMORROW'S WORLDS　　　　**Edited by Robert Silverberg**
Personally chosen stories portraying tomorrow's worlds, each
written by an acknowledged master of the field. **AN0793—95¢**

FUTURE TIMES THREE　　　　　　　　　　**Rene Barjavel**
Here is a fantastic journey that takes you from the past to the
year 300,000 A.D. One of the most unusual science-fiction
novels ever written!　　　　　　　　　　　　　　**AS0743—75¢**

THE DEMONS OF SANDORRA　　　　　　　**Paul Tabori**
In this brilliantly conceived work of shattering impact, voyage
only two centuries into the future—to find a world gone mad!
　　　　　　　　　　　　　　　　　　　　　　　AS0716—75¢

GODS FOR TOMORROW　　**ed. by Hans Stefan Santesson**
Ten science fiction masterpieces grapple with problems of
faith as new as tomorrow . . . as old as time. Chillingly brilliant.　　　　　　　　　　　　　　　　　　　　**AX0240—60¢**

Probe the Unknown

THE ABOMINABLE SNOWMEN   Eric Norman

Proof that these incredible creatures exist in well populated areas of the United States . . . authenticated eye-witness accounts of nature's wierdest phenomenon. This book may well be the most thorough study on the incredible Abominable Snowmen.   AS0479—75¢

THE SKY PEOPLE   Brinsley Le Poer Trench

In this astounding but scholarly book you will find proof that visitors from other planets exist—and that they are among us now!   AS0706—75¢

STRANGERS FROM THE SKIES   Brad Steiger

Why has the Air Force—after years of silence—suddenly announced an "intensive investigation" of flying saucer data? A fascinating in-depth report—astonishing quotes from eye witnesses.   AX0171—60¢